BLACK RAGE

By

LUMIERE BUKASA

Contents

Lumiere Bukasa

STRENGTH OF A BLACK WOMAN

Part 1

When Niah forgot the tunes of her mother's tongue, she would crawl in between her mother's legs, curl up, anxiously waiting for her mother's hymns and hair treatment. At times, she sipped from her steaming hot tea cup while sitting on the Tuscany rug her father gifted her. She remembered her mother always telling her, "Naw, mama Niah! You is working too hard. Look at you, very hazy. You gotta rest sometimes, baby." Her mother's eyes inspected every inch of her. Niah gazed at her mother fondly and replied, "Mama, I ain't gonna stop working until you get better." Her pledge was returned with a denial from her mother which startled Niah. "And what if I don't get better, you gon' work your whole life?" Niah remained silent pondering on this soul-stirring thought, knowing that her mother may not live long enough to see her grow. But Niah vowed in her heart to continue working. Her mother gazed upon the waning smile of Niah, and the shadow of light that danced between her eyes, "I suppose so" Niah vaguely replied. But then she wondered, what if her mother didn't get well? She brushed aside the jarring thought, as she prepared for her toil. Every penny she collected went into a jar for her mother's chemotherapy.

Once Niah made enough money to help, she gleefully hurried to the hospital where her mother stayed. When she arrived, she saw her mother laying in the hospital bed, her face losing color and her hand feeble.

Niah felt heat rising within her when she continued to pray, *"Mama, please get better, God please make mama better. I ain't got much strength left in me to fight. My body is tired. I ain't got much strength to give. My strength ain't there no more. Mama, please get better."* After she went to the hospital to pay her mother's treatment, she rushed home to make supper for her mother. She made gumbo because she knew her mother loved it.

She always remembered her mother's recipe. At times she remembered her mother's voice in the kitchen during the hot air of Louisiana's summer "Remember, gumbo is a stew thickened with roux and made with chicken or sausage. Nah, I luh me some sausage in my gumbo. The key is the roux, the flour, and oil. If you wanna make the best gumbo, you need to make sure the roux is cooked and stirred just right baby. If you want a deep rich gumbo, you need to make sure the roux is done well, you understand Niah." Niah would nod and continue to watch her mother cook.

She sat on the dining room chair ruminating on her mother's lively presence in the kitchen. The only sound she heard in the kitchen was of the simmering food in the pot and the humming from the gas stove's fire. Niah felt that this silence was eccentric. She dropped her head on the dining room table and yelled, "God, I ain't finna do this no more! Please heal ma mama!" She cupped her hands to snatch the tears that streamed from her eyes before they reached the table. Her mother always said that God never fails and this was the time for God to prove himself.

When the gumbo was done, she placed it in a bowl and wrapped it up for her mother. She threw on her trench coat and ran to the bus stop. After forty-five minutes of traveling, she arrived at the hospital to see her mother. She entered her mother's room, and her mother cheerfully hissed, "Aww, ma baby!" After greeting her mom, she handed the lunch bag that contained the bowl of gumbo. "Mama, I brought your favorite!" Once her mother opened the bag, her smile grew even wider, and exclaimed "My favorite! You brought my favorite food! I love you, baby. Thank you so much. God bless you, Mama Niah." Then she kissed Niah's forehead. There was a stillness, and Niah locked eyes with her mother. Niah looked at the unwavering smile on her mother's face while the sun from the window shed light into the room; her graying skin, dry lips, and her bald head were more visible than before. The hospital felt like a hospice, and Niah feared her mother would never leave alive.

Niah squeezed her eyes to stop the stream of tears she felt brewing. *Working to see a smile on my mama's face is worth all the hassle,* she thought. "Baby, please pass me the fork," her mother asked. Niah took the silver fork and handed it to her. She sat across from her mother, examining her mother's fading color. Her mother became pale. Her mother was never a person this pale. She remembered how her mother wore her afro with pride. When she felt stylish she would leave the pick in her afro, wore red lipstick, and carried herself graciously. Her mother was the epitome of black girl magic. But now, she became glued to the hospital bed with all of her hair gone and dulled skin.

The light and exuberance faded away. Smiles were hard to spot in that moment, but she flashed one when Niah asked, "How long will you be in here? How long will you suffer like this? What have the doctors said?"

4

Her mother put the fork down and hollered, "Baby, soon. God willing, but I ain't scared of nothing. I don't want you to be scared either. You understand? Fear paralyzes. Love and peace are liberating. I got love and peace for you, your brother, your sister, and your daddy. I need you to let go of fear and hold on to love and peace, baby. Everything will be alright."

Niah couldn't resist the urge to cry. "But Mama, why hasn't daddy been here to see you since you got here? Brother's gone, and I don't know where the hell he is."

"Young lady, you will watch your mouth" Niah's mother exclaimed. "Sorry mama. But my sister's gone too, your daughter mama. They supposed to be helping too. But ain't nobody caring for you, Mama. I ain't sure what love to give them."

"You must love them, baby." Niah responded with a stubborn yet lovely tone. "Baby love them. I ain't love them because they gave me a reason to love. They ain't giving me a reason to love them, but baby--- I love them because love liberates. When I chose to love them, my heart removed them from my mental prison. That liberated me. I hold nothing against them. They are my children and my husband." Niah's mother was smoother than a stick of butter placed on a hot pan. Niah's mother continued to glare at her daughter, then flashed a quick warming smile "Now come here and get some gumbo. You sure are throwing it down baby. Ain't this good!" Niah smiled at her mother's compliment. After a while, Niah rose from her seat to head home. After their warming goodbyes, Niah took the bus back home. When the bus stopped at her place, she rushed to her quiet and gloomy room. After Niah settled, she heard a knock at the door. The knocking quickly turned into banging, then someone yelled, "Maya! You better open this damn door!

"I ain't playing with you, woman!" The man continued to frantically and aggressively bang the door shouting for Maya, Niah's mother. Niah calmly walked to the door and answered. The guy on the other side of the threshold stared at Niah from head to toe and squealed, "Hey baby, how are you doing? You grown nah? Where is your momma?" Niah's father tried to sound compassionate, but she saw through his pretense.

Without notice, Niah's father suspiciously plodded into the house, and his eyes frantically examined the room as if he expected to see a ghost. Niah kept silent, then he raised his voice at Niah with aggression, "Little girl, I asked you a question! Where your mama at?" Her father's six feet one inch height shadowed her. He dragged his heavy feet on the floor, cracking his knuckles. And for a second, Niah saw his muscles jutting out his tight white long sleeve shirt as if he was ready for war.

"Why do you care, daddy?" Niah finally responded. Her father's eyes poked out, and Niah could see an angry smirk on his face "Excuse me young lady?" He clamored.

Niah flipped her wrist and replied "You're excused daddy." While she backpedaled, her father yelled, "Little girl, don't play with me! I ain't one of your lil friends. I'll beat your ass! I asked you a damn question. Where yo mama at?"

Flashbacks of her father's violent past and his irate demeanor caused quivers down her spine. She hopelessly vented, "Why do you care, Daddy? You left us. It's been a year. We don't know where you've been. You left us with no money and nothing to take care of ourselves! You left when mama got sick, and now she's worse than before. When she needed your support the most, you left. You ain't no, man daddy! I'm working to care for Mama. You left, Angie left, and Will left!" Niah always blamed herself for her brother Will's absence and her sister Angie's disappearance.

Her father's jaw flew to his chest when he was informed that his other kids left as well. Niah continued, "Y'all left mama to die. I'm working daddy, cleaning people's dishes. Ain't I a child daddy. Now here you are, tryna check on her. For what daddy-- cause you need cash?" Before Niah could finish her sentence, she felt an agonizing slap to her check that sent her plunging on the floor.

Niah fell on the floor, holding fast to her shirt, while her father used her head as a resting stool for his large foot. He continued to bark at her, "Don't you ever talk to me like that little girl! I'll beat you up just like I did your momma when she tried her bullshit." He cleared his throat and emptied his mouth by spitting on her while she laid on the ground. When her father saw that Niah's mother was not in the house he pulled his long sleeve shirt, sighed and leaped out the home. "You and yo mama can go to hell! You ain't my responsibility to take care of! I got other kids." Before he walked out the door, he spit in the home, still gazing at Niah's body laying on the floor

Her father never embodied the role of being the breadwinner. Without Niah, the house was in shambles. Niah's siblings and mother never tasted the fruits of his labor. Niah grew up hating her father, her sister Angie, and her brother Will. Her mother told her to love them, but how could she love them? They didn't care for her or her mother's wellbeing. At times she wondered if she was truly related to them.

Niah picked herself up, wiped her tears, and changed her clothes. Even though Niah didn't think much of her father, she couldn't believe he spat on her.

In the morning, Niah woke up at 5:00 AM and prepared herself for work at her first job until midday. After washing dishes for neighbors, she went to clean houses in the evening until late in the evenings which were reserved for visiting her mother.

One day, when she went to the hospital, she spotted the doctor holding her mother's hand and telling her something which she felt was serious. Her nerves bubbled while she watched from the squared glass window in between the wooden door. When Niah walked into the room, the doctor turned away and left, avoiding eye contact with her. "Hey, Mama," Niah uttered. Her mother smiled at Niah, but her face turned cold when she spotted bruises on her face, her mother asked, "Baby, what happened? Don't tell me you were fighting. I didn't raise you to fight. What happened, baby?"

Niah hesitated, "I fell, Mama. I was getting off the bus and slipped. I know, that was irresponsible of me." She still remembered the slap from her father that caused her to bruise. But she concealed this from her mother. She knew her mother would be hurt if she heard that her father bruised her as she was an animal.

Her mother took a breath of relief and sighed, "Be careful, baby. I still need you." "Thanks, Mama. Why was the doctor here?" Niah asked. Her mama looked at her and responded, "Ohh, that was nothing. He just wanted to check to see if I'm getting better."

"Are you getting better mama?" Niah interjected. Her mother paused and replied, "God willing." Niah pried, knowing her mother hid something from her. The evening quickly turned into night, and Niah left the hospital.

Niah's life became an excruciating experience, and she dreaded each day. One day Niah visited her mother in the hospital, and she saw that her mother's condition was not getting any better. Her mother would then say, "Niah, I want you to remember something. No matter what happens, I love you, your brothers, and your daddy. Your daddy isn't always easy to understand, but he is a good man, always remember that. Remember that you are a strong beautiful black woman. You can carry the world on your back and do it so graciously. Remember, you have always been a hefty woman, and you don't need anyone's love except for God's. Continue being strong." Niah's face crumpled in confusion. She knew her father wasn't a good man, but wondered why her mother defended his actions. Her father would beat her and her mother, and at times he was never home.

She sat next to her mother and saw the little strength her mother had dwindling like a candlelight at the end of its life. Her mother smiled at her as a tear leaked down the left side of her face right before she took her final breath. Niah desperately shook her mother and screamed. Doctors rushed in, but it was too late. Two nurses dragged Niah outside of the room as she continued to scream. They pulled Niah outside and locked the door behind her. Niah banged on the window while her mother flatlined. The doctors worked tirelessly to resuscitate her mother but to no avail. Before she knew it, the doctors took the sheet and covered her face. Niah watched her mother being transported to the morgue in disbelief. Her deepest fear manifested right before her eyes. She was motherless and fatherless in a snap of time.

In the following weeks, Niah continued working and exacerbating the little strength she had left. Her father and siblings did not attend her mother's funeral. Niah worked twice as hard, sold everything in the house, and went days without eating to bury her mother. She begged in the streets, asked her mama's friends for support until she had enough to pay for her mother's burial. Others would say, *let the dead, bury the dead* as if support was a hard thing to give. The thought of not hearing her mother's voice again shattered her heart every time it surfaced. At the funeral, she couldn't walk toward the coffin to see her mother's dull and lifeless face.

"You're brave, Niah. You are strong and ain't no child like you. You are your mother's daughter." Her mother's friends would say. Some would ask, "Where is yo daddy at? Where is yo sista at? Where is your brotha at?" She wanted to know where they were just as badly as they wanted to know.

Niah would often plead to the sky, "Mama, I'm sorry. I'm sorry that the children you carried abandoned you. I'm sorry the man you gave everything to left when you needed him the most. Mama, I hope you ain't crying while you're in your grave. I hope you ain't tossing and turning in pain in your grave. I promise you I'll work until you are well. I promise."

People cried at her mother's burial. Her closest friends cried as if they lost their own blood. Niah lost all she had. She had no father, no sister, no brother. Just herself. Once the repast was over, one of her mother's friends wailed, "I just want to tell you that if you need anything, me and my husband are here, okay. We can take care of your needs, baby."

After the burial, everyone carried on with their lives without worry. However, Niah's life changed forever. She cried for days once her mother was laid six feet under. Niah hid herself in the house and ate a little less.

She remembered her mother's words. "Na, baby, you are beautiful, you know that, right? You are powerful. Ain't nobody like you, and that's your weapon. You can do anything if you put your mind to it, you understand?" Her mother was so tender and gentle, yet her words pierced through her like a double-edged sword. "You have always been a strong woman, baby. You are superhuman and can do anything." Once Niah gained enough strength to leave the house, she spotted bold red eviction notices on the door. The most recent one read, "Dear Tenant, you are hereby given an eviction notice to vacate the premises within 15 days. The reason for this eviction notice is for failure to pay your rent." At that moment, she understood that her mother passed away months ago. To her, it seemed like time stopped ticking.

Niah knew she couldn't pay the rent, immediately, she rushed inside the home to pack her belongings. She packed everything including her mother's brown torn leather covered bible.Her mother once told her, "Baby, my mama gave me this, and I carried it everywhere I went. One day, I'll give it to you." Her mother passed away before she had the chance to hand it over to her as a torch. But Niah took it as it reminded her of her mother's love.

Niah wandered, looking for a place to stay, after she fled her home. No family and friends had an open door waiting for her. One day during her venture, she vehemently rushed into a gas station desperate for help and water.

When she arrived at the cashier counter she pleaded to the cashier, "Excuse me, ma'am. My name is Niah. I am 15 years old. I ain't got no place to go, food, or water. Please help me with something to eat and drink. I ain't got nobody to help me. My mama died. My daddy, sista, and brotha gone."

"Where is your family?" The cashier asked. Niah hesitated, then answered, "My mama died months ago. I dunno where the rest of my so-called family is." She began tearing up and looked away to hide her pain.

"Alright, I'll give you some water and snacks, but I can't help you with shelter. I can give you a place that helps people okay" The cashier continued.

"How old did you say you are, hun?"

"Fifteen ma'am, but I'm turning 16 soon," Niah replied as her knees trembled.

The lady ripped a piece of paper from her notebook, wrote an address and phone number, then handed it to Niah, along with some snacks, a bottle of water, some change to use for the bus, and a map. The cashier explained the directions to Niah, and Niah felt a love she hasn't felt in months.

The directions led to a homeless shelter. She walked into the gate and went to the front desk, and when someone spotted her, they summoned her to draw near.

"Hello, what can I do for you young lady?"One of the workers at the shelter asked.

Niah retold her story to the worker. Then the lady handed her a clipboard with documents to fill out. Niah's reading was subpar, but the lady helped her fill out the forms. Once she was done, the lady walked her to a cot, handed her blankets and sheets. She did not find comfort in that cot, but still held onto a flickering hope her mother left her with. She missed her mama's soft bed, her knitted blanket, the warmth of the burning candle in her room. As the night went on, more ladies her age and a little older came into the building. Niah curled up tightly under the paper-thin blanket. She thought to herself, *this ain't home. My mama is gone, my home is gone. I'm homeless. HOMELESS.* Those words were embedded in her mind, and the more she thought of them, the more she became numb. "Mama, please come home. Your baby is homeless," she whispered to herself before plummeting into sleep.

Life went on, and she grew accustomed to being homeless. She woke up, ate her breakfast, went about her day, then returned to the shelter at night. Niah grew interested in magazines and books, and the lady at the front desk gave her many. Eventually, she became friends with a woman named Beatrice, who was three years older. Beatrice was a tall girl with a curvy figure. Her hair was always in a messy bun, and she always wore black leggings with a white or pink polo shirt. Beatrice told Niah stories, read to her, and helped improve her reading and writing. Beatrice became the sister Niah never had.

Time passed and Beatrice started asking Niah questions about her past. Niah's past caused her to be nostalgic, but she felt that Beatrice deserved to know her past.

"Where did your sister go?" Beatrice asked.

"I dunno. She did crack, got an awful boyfriend, got pregnant, and left. Mama didn't want her to leave, but she left and never came back." Niah continued.

"Do you miss her?"Beatrice pressed.

Niah remained quiet questioning herself. She convinced herself that she hated her sister until that moment. "Yeah. I miss my brotha and my daddy too, but I ain't never forgiving them. They did my mama wrong. When my mama needed them, they left and she died."

When Niah grew emotional about discussing her past, Beatrice would change the subject. Their bond deepened as they did each other's hair, hung out on the streets, and spent time in the shelter. Beatrice's care reminded Niah of her mother's.

Niah relied on Beatrice for almost everything. When Niah was in the shelter without Beatrice, she would lay flat on her stomach, reading and waiting for Beatrice. She would not sleep until she saw Beatrice walk into the shelter. When Niah turned 18, Beatrice helped her get a job and educated her on everything. Beatrice reawakened Niah's hope for family, until she was killed in a car accident.

Part 2

There was a loud knock on the door that awakened Niah from a shivering episode and a nightmare. When she woke up, she realized she had another episode as her mind revisited her past. Once Niah realized she overslept, she began rushing to fix the bed and get ready. A note fell off the bed that read, *"Niah, I know it's hard, but I know that everything will be well. I am here to support you as a husband and as a best friend. I love you, baby."* It seemed that her husband knew she needed to hear those words after the night's scuffle.

After the much needed moment, her daughter, Ujamma called for her in the kitchen downstairs. Niah dressed and rushed downstairs. "How did you sleep baby?"Niah kissed her daughter's forehead and pulled the glass of water closer to Ujamaa.

Ujamaa ignored her imploration, "Good, but mama, you woke up late. And you look tired." Niah fixed Ujamaa's hair into two ponytails, and nonchalantly answered, "I'm fine baby. Nah, you eat fast. Go on, get your shoes. Let me drop you off at school, I gotta be at the shop in 30 minutes."

After dropping her daughter at school, Niah drove to her beauty salon. Maya's Beauty. Each time she walked into the shop, she smirked that her salon is a legacy of her mother. *"Mama, I did it for you. I told you I'd work until you got well."* Niah opened a beauty shop in her neighborhood to honor her mother and serve her community. Her beauty shop was named after her mother.

Business was always moderate. Women came in for braid-ins, to buy products, and to socialize. Nineties R&B, jazz always played in the background. Women from the neighborhood came to her shop to buy products, get their hair done, socialize, gossip, laugh and listen to stories.

After work Niah drove to pick up Ujamaa from school. When they arrived home, Niah darted to the kitchen to prepare supper. She took out fresh collard greens from the fridge and other ingredients for gumbo.

After they settled in the kitchen, Niah began doing her daughter's hair. Once Ujamaa became comfortable in her mother's lap she would ask her mother questions not fit for a child to ask, "Mama, someone at school told me that my skin is too dark and that it would look better if I was mixed. Is something wrong with my skin?" Niah put the comb down, her mind froze for only a second, "No, baby, ain't nothin wrong with you. You are beautiful, inside and out. In fact, you are the cutest little girl I know." Then, she pinched Ujamaa's cheeks, and they chuckled.

After a few moments of silence Niah asked, " Ujamaa, why would you think your skin is too dark?" Ujamaa paused, fumbling with her hands and crossing her feet."Because these girls in school always make fun of my hair and say it's ugly. They'll make jokes about my skin." Niah felt an anger gashing through her body and her stomach growled.

"They always make fun of me." Ujamaa continued. Ujamaa was nine years old and a replica of Niah. Her almond-shaped eyes held a hazel brown tinge to it, and when different hues of light reflected in them, they would reveal unique shades of brown. Ujamaa was just as

16

slim as her mother, and when she smiled, her cheeks would reveal dimples that Kuumba loved. Her eyebrows were full, and she was a little girl with a lot of hair, just like Niah.

Ujamaa's words revived memories of Niah's childhood and the bullying she faced. Niah held back the frown and smiled at her daughter, "You are beautiful, baby. It's sad that some people will never see it because they don't want to, but ain't nothin wrong with you. God made you unique baby. You understand?" Niah encouraged Ujamaa, but Ujamaa did not believe her words. She interjected, "But mama, look at my hair." Ujamaa touched her thick 4c hair and continued, "You take a long time to make it soft, and even when it gets soft for one minute, the next, it's nappy. And it doesn't look good like the other girls in my class. Those girls have straight hair. Even the teacher. You should straighten my hair." Ujamaa grew to believe her hair not as good as the other girls in her class

"Your hair is beautiful, from the coils in your hair, to the kinks, to the shrinkage, to the afro. Everything about your hair is just as beautiful as the next, darling. Beauty comes in a variety. Their beauty isn't yours, that doesn't mean you are less beautiful. Don't measure your beauty to another person. Otherwise, you'll always think you are not good enough, you understand baby." Niah snapped.

She continued oiling Ujamaa's scalp but different thoughts raced through her mind. "Ujamaa, my mama used to always tell me something that I'mma pass to you. She would say, Niah, become so secure in yourself that uplifting another person does you no harm. Only a person who does not know their worth will hesitate to uplift another person. Those that are low want others to be low with them. She is her own beauty in her white skin, as you are beautiful in your black skin, and the most important beauty is your heart, not your skin. All skin is beautiful, you understand, baby?" Niah paused, waiting for Ujamaa's response. "Yes, Mama."

There was still prickly silence, and Niah continued combing, moisturizing, and twisting Ujamaa's hair. "Mama, so I'm beautiful, right?" Ujamaa implored. Niah looked into mere space, reminiscing of her childhood traumas, the self-hatred that society tried to instill in her due to the perception of black skin. Thankfully, her mama uprooted those negative self-images like bad weeds in a garden. Niah gently ran the comb in Ujamaa's hair, remembering how her mama used to do it. Memories came flashing in her mind. She remembered the yellow comb her mama used, the gentleness of her hands, and the shea butter she plastered over her kinks. Moments such as this quenched the depressive fire that existed in her.

Niah recited a poem she wrote for Ujamaa when she was born, knowing that moments like this would come. "As the moon holds its own beauty, so do you, my love. I want you to appreciate the rich inherited melanin in your skin, the plumpness in your lips, the span of your hips, the roundness that will come, the copper-like, sun-kissed, and marinated skin. Ujamaa, my love, your skin is a victim of constant abuse, neglect, and inferiority. Just because society sees your skin as inferior, does not mean you are, my love. Inferiority is a mindset and what people call you, but it's not what you are. You don't have to conform to what they call you, my love. You choose who you want to be and how you want to see yourself. You are beautiful, but if you cannot see it, then if a person tells you you're ugly, you will say you are because you don't know who you are."

Niah continued to run the golden Afro hair pick in Ujamaa's 4c hair. Ujamaa plopped down in between her mama's feet, watching a cartoon show. Her mama took the oil applicator bottle and smeared oil onto Ujamaa's scalp, twisted it, and placed a golden satin bonnet on her hair. Niah kept oiling Ujamaa's scalp then the door cracked.

A man slightly above six feet tall walked into the house with a slouched frame. "Daddy!" Ujamaa yelled after noticing her father's presence. She ran up into his arms, hugged her father and took his bag away.

Niah sat down, watching the scene unfold with a grin on her face and black circles under her eyes. This was something she never had, but she was glad her children had it. She waited for Ujamaa to stop interrogating her father before going to wrap her arms around him. "Daddy look! Mama did my hair." Ujamaa pulled her rose gold bonnet off, showcasing the twists, then her father proudly exclaimed, "I bet your curls will be poppin tomorrow, baby girl." Niah interjected, "Okay, Ujamaa, go on in your room for homework. Leave your father alone so he can rest." Ujamaa conformed and bolted upstairs to her room. Before she made it to the staircase, Niah walked to Kuumba, then they hugged and kissed.

"Welcome home, Kuumba," she whispered to him, soaking in his aroma, and wrapping her hands around his neck. "Thank you, my love. How are you feeling?" he replied, smiling at her while gazing deeply into her eyes. "I'm feeling much better after taking the herbs and vitamins." Then they walked to the kitchen area, and Kuumba sat down, studying his wife's movements. It's been a while since he's seen her in the kitchen. Niah grew accustomed to hiding in an empty room, sobbing and writing in her journal. Kuumba offered to help with the cooking as Niah was still recovering. The doctors claimed it would take years for Niah to accept the nightmare of her lost child and heal from her past trauma.

Niah smiled, exposing her crooked teeth and a golden tooth at the side of her mouth. "You can cut those vegetables in the sink and wash those dishes while you're at it. Please, and thank you." Niah kissed Kuumba then walked away from him.

"Yes, ma'am," Kuumba smiled. He rolled up his sleeves and began working. "So, how was your day, queen?" Kuumba asked.

"It went well. I went to the shop. It was kind of slow, but the girls helped pass the time. Stephanie's mom stopped by to buy braids for her daughter, and her white friend Linda had braids as too. They looked cute."Niah chuckled

"Oh really. She rocked em?" he chuckled.

"Yes, but she received a lot of backlash from other ladies. I mean I get it."

"That's funny. I bet them women who be comin' there had something to say?" Kuumba tittered. "Umm, lemme tell you." Niah cackled "I felt terrible for the poor girl. Keisha was like, 'Oh, I know you lyin'. This white chick really thinks she's rockin 'em. She lookin' like one of those white bitches who only like black men."

Kuumba burst in laughter, "Keisha's crazy."

"Yeah, but she helps pass time. She knows everybody's business but her own. This girl is updated on the latest gossip, on everybody's life. I hope she is just as updated on her own. Anyway, how was your day? Tell me about it." Niah asked.

20

"I had a long day at work. I spoke to several inmates about forgiveness before rehabilitation because I believe rehabilitation starts with forgiveness and the changing of self. I noticed that there was a lot of unforgiveness among the inmates. Some are angry with their fathers for not being there. Some were angry at themselves, some were angry at the white man, some at the system, and some at their families. I told them that forgiveness is at the core of emotional, spiritual, and physical healing, and they cannot have true rehabilitation without the element of forgiveness. When you hold bitterness in your heart, you infect your heart with an illness that will destroy your life. Forgiveness helps with removing the shackles and getting out of mental imprisonment. God called us to forgive and to love those who hate us. He loved those who hated him, and if you look in the book of Colossians 3:13, we see that God commands us to forgive each other as God has forgiven us. Forgiveness is key to self-liberation, Niah." Kuumba finished cleaning all the dishes and soaked in the food's aroma. Niah began setting the table with the plates, towels, and glasses of water.

Niah locked eyes with her husband while smirking at him and admitted, "That's a much-needed message for everyone." She knew that she was no different from those inmates, as she needed to forgive too. They continued cooking. Niah mixed the sausage, roux, and rice for the gumbo. Kuumba cut the collard greens and took the beans from the fridge.

"I spoke to a young man named Jaylen. He's 28 years old and was given eight years in prison for burglary of multiple felonies. I heard his story, how his father was never there for him. He lost everything and dropped out of school. His father was always in and out. He was quiet during our session. The only thing he uttered was, *Ain't nobody ever gonna care. My father wasn't there to care, so ion expect nobody to care.* He was charged with multiple offenses and sent to prison. He has a board hearing coming up in the next few weeks. I'm hoping they don't judge him based on his past mistakes." Kuumba uttered.

"Baby, I know it frustrates you, but you'll be alright. You give people like Jaylen hope to know people care." Niah exposed her crooked smile. Kuumba glanced at her smile and felt protection and saw an intimate sanctuary for his soul. He asked, "What would I do without you, my love?" They both smiled, shared a kiss, and continued cleaning and making dinner.

They finished cooking and placed everything on the table, right before Titus and Zaire walked through the door. "Hey Mama, hey Daddy," they both uttered. Titus was a slim, ten-year-old boy with chestnut-colored skin and a smile that could light up a room. He looked like his father, with his wide nose, kinky coils, and a rugged demeanor. Niah always reminded Titus that he looked and acted like his father.

Zaire was more like his mother. He was an eighteen-year-old boy who thought he knew everything. Zaire was very argumentative, tall like his father, and had his mother's ebony rich skin. He was artistically talented and always played the guitar in his room after school.

After they kissed their parents on the cheek before heading upstairs, Kuumba shouted, "Dinner is in thirty minutes. Go on, get ready before dinner."

"Daddy, that's not enough time to get ready," Titus pleaded and both Kuumba and Niah ignored his plea. They knew Titus loved to take his time.

Before Titus could say anything else, Kuumba cut him off, "Y'all should have thought of that before y'all came home late. Go on, get ready. Y'all have thirty minutes."

"Daddy, you know how the barbers are. Mr. Anthony took an hour to cut my hair. He ordered food, ate, talked on his phone, even took a nap too. But he did me right, though." Everyone shared a laugh then the boys proceeded to get ready for dinner.

Once they made it to the kitchen table thirty minutes later, Kuumba muttered, "I'm glad y'all respected the time." Titus replied, "I know you and Mama don't play about family dinner."

Niah replied, "That's right. Now, Ujamaa, would you care to bless our food? Everybody hold hands." Kuumba closed his eyes, but he did not believe in prayers or a God. The youngest of the family pleaded, "Let's pray. Father God, please bless the food. Please bless Mama and Daddy for buying and preparing the food. Please bless my brothers so that next time they come home on time." Niah and Kuumba squinted and smirked at each other until the prayer was over, and they all said Amen. "Alright, Mama. Please pass the gumbo," Titus exclaimed after the prayer.

Then titters rose, along with laughter. After dinner, the family continued telling stories about their day, school, and work. Time passed, and the night crept in before they realized. Niah took Ujamaa to bed, as she was sound asleep. She sat at the edge of Ujamaa's bed, massaging her head and stroking her back. Rubbing her daughters' back helped her omit the thoughts of her lost baby. Niah had a miscarriage a year before, and that haunted her.

She decorated a room with blue wallpaper, a cradle, and a rocking chair, with a pastel blue blanket next to Ujamaa's room when she was pregnant. When she lost her child, she could not believe reality. Niah sulked in the empty room periodically. Although this was not good for her because it was mentally draining, she still found comfort in the room. After a while, Niah left the room and traveled to her son's room where Kuumba was.

"Daddy, how's your counseling going?" Zaire questioned. "Well, counseling is going well. I counseled a boy named Jaylen today. He's preparing for parole, and I'm trying to help him through it. He has a lot of built up anger and doesn't have a positive outlook on life because that's all he knows. If he leaves the prison like this, he's gonna go right back."

"What did Jaylen do wrong?" Titus inquired as he drew invisible lines in the palm of his hands. Niah turned the doorknob and entered the room before Kuumba answered the question. She sat next to her husband and held his arm because she knew his mind was about to channel a grim moment.

"Well, son, when Jaylen was 20 years old, he was arrested. He lived in the worst hood of Nashville, Tennessee. He did not have a father figure in his life, and not a lot of men in his community were examples. He did all kinds of drugs, roamed the streets, met the wrong crowd, drank heavily, sold marijuana, robbed homes, cars, and anything. His mother had four kids, two by different men. They had problems affording the bare minimum and Jaylen rarely saw his father. His father had time for other women but never made time for him. Jaylen's mom spent many hours working as a seamstress but struggled providing, so Jaylen was mainly raised by the streets and grew up fast." As Kuumba told the story, Niah could see herself in Jaylen.

"One night, Jaylen roamed the city high and got drunk with his gang looking to rob people. Before they knew it, the police were on them like termites on bright lights during the springtime. It turned out the police were looking for that gang due to several misdemeanors and felony charges. They arrested Jaylen and his entire crew. He was in prison for five years, but no one ever visited him. His mama was heartbroken, but never showed her face. One of his siblings claimed it was his fate to be behind bars." Kuumba paused, then looked at Niah, who rested her head on his shoulder. Kuumba took his long arms and wrapped them around her. Titus and Zaire sat on their bunk beds as their feet shivered and hands cupped their faces.

Zaire commented, "Dang, that's really messed up. I hope he is good now," and Titus added a similar sentiment. Kuumba sniffled, "Oh yeah, he's good now. He will be let out soon, so we gotta help him when he leaves prison."

Kuumba believed that black men were needed in black communities such as Hadley, the one they lived in. He was a freedom fighter and spoke up against racial injustices. Kuumba was a firm believer that only black men can teach black boys in his community the importance of manhood and what it meant to be a man. He was a passionate leader that believed childhood was the most important time to reach young black males and prevent them from becoming misguided and criminalized. Kuumba always taught Zaire and Titus how to be men, respond to the police, behave, and become men of value. He believed it was the duty of the older black men to teach the younger generations. Kuumba thought most of his community's problems, such as single-parent homes, abuse, and neglect, would be solved if the men were taught manhood.

Zaire suggested, "Daddy, it's sad, but he got himself there, so he paid the price." Kuumba put his arm around Zaire and smirked, "Son, I agree. He did the time, and he paid for his wrongdoings, but his future shouldn't be hindered because of his past." Kuumba was a vigorous advocate of black unity and believed that America saw a crime committed by one black man as a reflection of the entire race. He continued, "When a black man sins, society makes it seem as if it represents the whole black race. Crime does not discriminate. When a black man commits a crime, it becomes criminalized and stigmatized." Zaire eagerly responded, "I see what you mean, Daddy, but isn't crime higher amongst black folks? I mean, we don't really talk about black on black crimes, but we steadily talk about crimes white folks do to us -" Kuumba cut him off and hung his train of thoughts in the room, "Sorry to cut you off, but that's how I see it. We gotta focus on fixing our community and lowering our crime rates, instead of saying white people doing this to us. You're smart son. I'm not disagreeing with you. I'm saying black equals crime in society's eyes. When one black person commits a crime, it's a community thing. However, when a white person commits crimes, it's an individual thing. Violence is terrible, but our institutions try to racialize crime for blacks but not whites. That's what I fight against."

"Man, this ain't fair!" Titus exclaimed. Niah gently touched his knee uprooting a once kept remorse, "Ain't nothin fair, baby, but you gotta work through it. You gotta change it but complaining about it won't fix anything. Your father is a perfect example to follow.

Kuumba exclaimed, " Zaire, Titus, I want you to promise me that you will work hard and support this community as much as you can. I want you to be educated in life. Speak up whenever you see something wrong. I want you to value your masculinity, power, and wit. I want you to remember that it is much better to set the standards than follow other people's standards. Me and your mama will always be here for you." Kuumba's voice turned chilly, stern, and fiery as he spoke. He continued, "Remember, power comes from being educated. Education is a lethal weapon. Jaylen thought violence was the answer, and it cost him years of his life and a stained reputation. Violence imprisons, and education liberates. You'll be feared more once you become educated. A sharper mind is sharper than the sharpest sword. You two can uplift Hagley Park by being educated. Don't assimilate to a hood mindset. Buy your hood and clean it up. You two are strong black boys that will become men one day. We live in a society that kills black boys, so they can take away black men because the best way to destabilize a black community is to remove the man. The best way to destroy black men is to kill them while they are tender. The best way to strengthen a black man is to strengthen them while young. That's our duty as your parents." Niah looked at Kuumba, knowing Kuumba set an example to her black boys.

Niah added, "Jaylen did not have a positive male role model and father figure such as your daddy, so please be grateful and learn from him." They both poured knowledge, love, and encouragement into their children for thirty more minutes, then began making their way back to their room. Before they exited the room, Titus inquisitively pleaded, "Umm, Mama, am I still intelligent, even though I have a D in math?" Niah turned the light back and snarled, "Son, you know you can do better than that. I need you to show your full potential. A D is not your full potential. The grading system does not define your intelligence, but that doesn't mean you can't work hard and exercise your full potential. Good night boys, say your prayers and sleep tight."

The boys said their goodnights and rolled themselves into their bed, covering their bodies with a wool blanket made by their mama. Kuumba and Niah walked into their room, climbed into their bed. Niah made her way to his chest then asked, "What's wrong, Kuumba?"

Kuumba sighed,"I am worried about these boys. I'm not the praying type, but I pray that they grow up and live to see their full potential. Each day I fear for their future and hope they beat the odds of becoming another statistic. I even ask for simple things, such as them making it home safely for dinner." Kuumba knew his fear was not exclusive, but synonymous. Black parents in America are meticulously haunted by nightmares of their sons and daughters not making it home for dinner. It is a piercing reality, a bête noire, a tormenting ordeal that seems to last longer than wanted. Everything under the sun has an expiration date, but this ordeal seemed unending. Kuumba was determined to end it and protect his children at all costs.

Niah interrupted his fears,, "Or they will end up like their father. A master graduate with two degrees fighting for justice and bringing light to his community." Although Kuumba could have leveraged his education economically, he decided to remain in his community to rebuild it.

Kuumba struggled to shake off his fears and smile, "Niah, I want to start an organization that helps black boys on parole integrate back into society once they leave prison. They have little to no resources. People like Jaylen need help once they leave prison. I have started the paperwork for the organization. Next week, I am hosting a gathering here to raise funds for the organization and raise awareness toward black inmates' inability to integrate back into reality after leaving prison." Kuumba continued. Niah rubbed the back of her husband's head and vowed that he had the family's support.

The night simmered, crickets sang their songs, and dreams wove into mental realities. Niah woke up in the middle of the night, going through one of her episodes. She plodded in a rocking chair in her baby's room and gazed at the light blue wallpaper, cradle, lamp in the distance, and blankets she wove while humming a tune.

She slipped into a deep state of hopelessness, once she spotted her mama's bible on the nightstand. Suicidal thoughts weren't foreign to her. She wended from her rocking chair to peel off the light blue wallpaper with tears in her eyes. A moment passed, and she felt as though she heard her mama's voice saying, "You always been a strong woman, baby. Ain't nobody ever gotten to you. You a superhuman."

Nia sulked across the rocking chair in the chilly and indolent room while humming a tune she hummed in her early pregnancy. Once she peered out the window, tears crept down her cheeks. This side of her was reserved for the darkness. Even when Niah didn't feel strong, her mother's affirmations gave her the strength to carry on and hide her pain from others. Many nights since the miscarriage were spent rolling on the floor in misery with her baby's blanket as the images of her childhood played back in her mind. Her daddy, beating her and spitting on her was one of the most replayed memories. She was the strength of everyone but herself. She cried over everything but couldn't reveal her wounds of the strong black woman she was.

She howled and spoke to herself as if she spoke to her mama. "Mama, I ain't got much strength in me to fight." She continued talking to herself until Kuumba walked into the room. "Niah! Niah!" he called his wife multiple times and realized she wouldn't respond. Kuumba approached her, held her, and helped her up. She cried to him, shivered, and jumped out of paranoia as if she feared someone was coming to harm her. Kuumba sat on the carpet next to her, placed his arms around her, and rocked her. After Niah calmed down she proclaimed, "Mama told me I'm strong. I'm a strong black woman. I don't need saving, but I can save. I thought I was strong, and I wanted to be strong, but I can't anymore. I am tired of being strong. I'm tired of being superhuman. Sometimes I just want to be a woman. Sometimes I want to be cared for, loved, and appreciated. I am tired of trying to save the world. I need saving too."

Kuumba held her tighter and whispered into her ear, "Baby, if you want, we can get you medical help." She defensively responded, "What for? I'm good all by myself. I can take care of myself." "I know," Kuumba responded, "but you gotta let people help you too." Before he could get another sentence out she screamed, "I'm good. I'mma be alright, just like mama."

Kuumba helped Niah up, but the night ended with her in the room. When the kids woke up, they questioned their mama's wellbeing. They scrutinized their daddy, and he replied, "Mama's good. She just needs to be left alone right now. Gon' on, get ready for school." Kuumba would help the kids get ready for school, cook for them, drive them to school, and drive to the Davidson County Correctional Development for counseling. Once he arrived, the inmates would gleefully greet him, except for Jaylen.

"Jaylen."

"Mr. Douglas." Kuumba and Jaylen greeted each other. Then he continued, "I know y'all had rough lives. I know I ain't gonna understand all of your struggles, but they are struggles that connect us all as black men in America. I want y'all to know I'm here for y'all."Kuumba Exclaimed.

After the session, Jaylen approached Kuumba and expressed his penitence, "Mr. Douglas, I'm sorry for how I behaved towards you during the past few days. It's just that my whole life, I've been alone, doing me, without correction, so I don't know how to handle it, but thank you for caring for me. Ain't nobody ever cared for me, and I appreciate you for that." Kuumba gleamed with mere joy as if the prodigal son had returned home.Then he responded, "Son, I'm here for you. I'm here to fight for you, prepare you for the real world. You'll get out of here. And I need you to be ready, son. You understand me, son?"

Jaylen fought back tears and moaned, "Yes sir."

Group therapy ended, and in the following weeks, Kuumba and Jaylen grew closer. The more Jaylen spoke about his family, the more Kuumba saw Niah in him. One day, they spoke about Niah and her past and how it aligned with Jaylen's. After hearing about Niah's story for the first time Jaylen knew she was a woman of her mother's strength, "She seems strong, Mr. Douglas. I hope I can meet her."

Kuumba nodded and assured Jaylen that one day, he will meet the love of his life. Kuumba knew Parole was approaching, and felt burdened to prepare Jaylen for his parole hearing. God, please let this boy come out of prison, Kuumba would silently pray before leaving prison.

Niah's episodes progressively worsened, and Kuumba was determined to find a solution for her. On a sunny Sunday morning, Niah rose from her traumatic sleep, showered, dressed, and put makeup on for church. She was an expert at masking her pain. They all hopped into the car and left for church, but before Niah left, she seasoned the meat, prepared rice, beans, and a casserole dish because Kuumba called a meeting at their home after church. Kiah knew her house would be packed, so she wanted everything to be on point. After church, they socialized, conversed, and smiled with the church members. While they rode back home, other church folks followed them.

When they got home, Niah changed her clothes, and rushed to the kitchen. Some church ladies came and helped. Niah cooked some southern soul food, and the aroma drew many smiling faces and happy dances from guests. Kuumba greeted everyone in the house then stepped outside to see if more people were coming. He saw more people running towards the house. As they reached the house, he greeted them with a hug and a handshake. Kuumba's uncles playfully sassed, "This shit better be good."

All the church members and community members filled their house, backyard, and front yard. "Alright, can I have everyone's attention, please?" Kuumba shouted over the murmurs, giggles, and gossip, "Thank you all for coming here today. As you all know, I'm a criminal psychologist and prison counselor. I have been working with black boys and men in jail to help counsel them. As you all know, black boys and men are incarcerated and given severe sentences. When they leave jail or prison, they have no help. I am starting an organization that will help these young black boys get counseling and transition back to reality. I need you as a community to support these black men. These people could be our brothers, nephews, uncles, cousins, or our sons."

Virtue, a nineteen year old boy eloquently explained life as if he was a walking library in the midst of people, "Y'all, I think supporting people like Kuumba and other brothas and sistas coming from the hood is important." Virtue was an ex-felon and ex-gang member who supported black unity. He continued, "They are trying to build something to bring justice to our community. Imagine if we owned our own rehabilitation center to help ex-convicts like myself and newly released inmates. We truly suffer trying to find jobs and get accepted in society."

"Ya know whenever we talk about tryna start something, we be all talk, but no action. I think what Kuumba's tryna do is good for the community. We gotta show our brothas and sistas leaving jail that they ain't alone." Raphial added. Raphial was Kuumba's father figure and mentor. Raphial's wife also mentored Niah.

"You ain't wrong, uncle Raphial. We can't talk without action. I believe we can do it, but faith without deeds ain't nothing. We must own things. That's one of the greatest ways for us to be free and help our people. Own our own entertainment industry, our own centers, our own everything. We gotta also create jobs and employ our people. Create jobs for black people, gain wisdom, and expose it to other black people. Stop arguing, and let's start doing. It starts with this meeting right here and Kuumba's rehabilitation center." Virtue replied.

"Boy, what do you know? You is nineteen," Uncle Raphial murmured. Virtue replied, "With all due respect, sir, I've been in jail, I've been on the streets, there is nothing I ain't done before, and I be observing the system. Them white folks know things about progress. I learned from them. If people like Kuumba have rehabilitation centers, that's gon save our brothas and sistas coming from jail or prison. A successful community needs excellent schools, hospitals, businesses, banks, markets, and good rehabilitation to rebuild and redirect those who've fallen.

We gotta support Kuumba and people like him." Virtue looked at Kuumba and sighed, "Hey man, I support you." Kuumba humbly nodded.

Kuumba, Raphial, and the others knew that a wise man leaves a legacy for their future generation. They all believed that the rehabilitation center could be a blueprint for generations to come and a haven for black inmates coming out of prison. Kuumba believed that jail was not a solution for reform. He believed counseling and rehabilitation centers were. He believed that rehabilitation centers gave black men their identity back because it gave them wisdom and knowledge of themselves. Kuumba held a mantra in life, which was, know thyself, and have a knowledge of your past, present, and future.

Once people in the crowd displayed supportive statements, Kuumba's voice overtook the crowd, and he affirmed, "I ain't gonna allow our boys, our men, or ourselves to be victims of the system! Hell, let's change things. Let's rebuild, help, and restore our brothers and sisters as they leave jail." Then everyone, even the children cheered and clapped. They all walked to the dining table with plastic plates, as they agreed to fund and raise funds for Kuumba's rehabilitation center. Kuumba smiled as his community brothers hugged him. Niah and the other women placed more food on the table as everyone gathered around the dining room. They talked and laughed as 90s music played in the background.

Everyone enjoyed the gathering except for Niah. She wanted to leave the state of hopelessness but did not know how. Her smiles couldn't make it from her mind to her face. She loved what Kuumba was doing, and wanted to show support, but how could she? Aside from the depression and internal harsh memories she was fighting, Niah noticed Raphial's wife scrutinizing her behind her back. Niah flared up and heard a negative voice in her head that intensified. She felt like she was in solitary confinement, even though she was around people. Kuumba noticed her energy was waning from across the room. He continued speaking to others while looking at her. Raphial's wife approached Niah.

"Baby, can I speak to you privately?" Raphial's wife asked in her soulful southern voice. Niah nodded then led her into the room of melancholy, hopeless dreams, and hopeless tries. Niah gestured for her to sit in the rocking chair by the bed. Raphial's wife refused and gave the chair to Niah, and she pulled out a gray upholstered bench to sit across from her. She looked at Niah for a while, and Niah felt the stare deeply probing her soul. "Nah, baby, how is you doing?" Niah claimed she was doing ok, but Raphial's wife didn't buy it. She compassionately rubbed Niah's hands and asked, "How are you holding up since your baby passed?" Niah licked her lips, lifted her head, and stared at the ceiling to prevent tears from escaping her eyes. Niah's baby died in the womb, so doctors had to remove it before it affected Niah, but Niah did not believe that her baby died.

Niah could not find the courage to speak or respond, so she gazed down at her discolored hands, smeared in rashness. Her mentor's forehead puckered, and eyes squinted as she stared at Niah vehemently then continued, "Baby, I know it's hard. I know it's hard to lose your baby. It's painful. I understand the pain you are going through." A flush of paleness overtook Niah's face, her expression dulled, and she pouted her lips as she rolled her eyes inward to stop the dancing water in her eyes. She waited for a few moments for Niah to say something then continued, I ain't never met a girl like you. I know you've always been strong and you didn't have time to ask nobody for help. You did it even before you left your mother's womb. You took care of your mama, you cooked, you cleaned, you dealt with your father and your siblings absence. It ain't easy. You had to always be the shoulder for people to cry on, and ain't nobody was there to be a shoulder for you until Kuumba came."

Niah wondered if she really understood her pain. Raphial's wife called out to her, but her voice seemed so far to Niah, and Niah felt like she was in a different universe being dragged back into reality.

Raphial's wife was in her late 50s and knew Niah from church. She was like a mother to Niah, and Niah confided in her. Raphial's wife always advised Niah, and Niah couldn't lie to her because she read Niah like a book. Niah never told her the specifics about her childhood trauma, but Raphial's wife understood that her childhood was the biggest nightmare that haunted her. She always told Niah,

36

"Baby, I'm praying for you. I know God will heal you and bless you."
Niah would always nod and smirk at her words.

"Baby, I know you is strong, but you can't be strong for foreva."
Raphial's wife gleamed with hope for Niah. After a while of lecturing,
Niah cried her heart out, and rested her head on Raphial's wife. Once
she gained enough strength she squealed, "I got beautiful kids and a
beautiful husband. They make me happy, but I cannot forget who I've
lost. I lost too much, Mama. As a woman, I always felt that I had to
rise above orchestrated unfairness placed on me. I had to fight my
way in school. I had to fight to prove myself. I had to fight to be seen
as strong in a world that degraded me and was unfair to me. Now, I
don't think I have any more fight in me to give. I'm tired, Mama."
"Baby, you ain't the only one. As black women, we are expected to
be strong and carry the entire world on our backs, even when we're
suffering. Sometimes carrying the burden of a thousand alone can
cause more heartache than a heroine story. You can't save the whole
world and leave yourself behind child. I need you to seek help for
your mental state, baby."

Niah did not understand why she found peace and comfort in the
smile of Mrs. Tabia, Raphial's wife of 30 years and a devoted woman
of God. She carried the bible wherever and preached the gospel
whenever given a chance. She partook in many civil rights
movements in America and fought for the rights of black women. She
was a firm devotee of praying and counseling, and she encouraged
Niah to do both.

My mental state? Ain't I fine? Niah thought. She couldn't say
anything. She never knew what "help" that was. She did everything
on her own and even shut down her husband's help. Tabia saw the

weariness in her face then pleaded, "Please get help baby. The strength and weakness of black women is always keep on keepin on. Keep on, keepin on, can tire you and wear you out baby. Sometimes you gotta let go. Learn to allow yourself to be vulnerable. Vulnerability is strength. Vulnerability is beautiful. We all need it, and we all need a shoulder to lean on when we ain't strong." Tabia sat back, simpering while caressing Niah's right arm. The yellow floral ribbon in Tabia's hair flickered each time she moved her body as if light was dancing in between the threads. After Tabia finished talking, she sat down quietly, allowing all she planted in Niah to sink in

Tabia began humming a tune and dribbled these words to Niah as a token of honor, "The strength of black women is beautiful, powerful, unmatched, and resilient." She paused, gave Niah a slight tap on her right arm, and continued. "But society gives black women no room to be vulnerable. The black woman seems to do it all. This toxic idea of strength and resilience wraps black women in silent struggles and constant stoicism. It's unhealthy, baby. Strength doesn't always mean I got my shit together, but it could be admitting you need help. Nah, baby, that's strength." Tabia was a devoted Christian but also cussed a little. People assumed she was not holy enough to spread the gospel, but she did not care and continued preaching and speaking her truth.

Niah halted her wailing, and she felt herself wrestling with leaving this state of hopelessness and mental confinement. Tabia wrapped her arms around Niah and hugged her. Once they expressed their love for each other, they made their way back to the party.

Several hours later, everyone left with to-go plates and drinks. After everyone left, the family cleaned the house and laughed as they retold the stories from earlier. Once the kitchen and living room was presentable, the kids strolled to their bedrooms and locked their doors to avoid cleaning more. Niah and Kuumba concluded the night shortly after they finished cleaning.

The following days, Niah's episode worsened. When her mental episodes inflamed, Niah would lock herself in her baby's room, speaking to the voices in her head, rolling, and turning as the voices intensified. Once she returned to reality, she would clean herself, cook, and try distracting herself with a television show or a book, or the bible.

Niah stayed home for a couple of days to recover, and Kuumba would open and close Niah's shop to keep business going. When employees would inquire about Niah, he'd say she was sick. After that, Kuumba would run errands and meet with a CPA to fill out paperwork for his organization. He filed the articles of incorporation and the bylaws and paid the CPA to submit his papers. Kuumba contacted organizations that did similar work with newly released inmates to find collaborators and partners. He attained many business partners, some of which offered him a place and an office in their building to do his work. As he continued to work, he prayed for Jaylen's release. He would also pray for Niah and somehow believed God would heal her. God, I ain't got much to give ya, but please heal my wife and release Jaylen. He would always pray. Kuumba did not believe in God wholeheartedly, but the more he worked in prison and spoke to Jaylen, his faith grew like a mustard seed. One day, as Kuumba prepared himself for work, he tramped outside, coffee in one hand, a briefcase in the other, his phone rang. He waited until he opened his car door to place the briefcase in the back seat before answering the call. "Hello?" He answered.

"Hey, Mr. Douglas. What ya up to?" The croaky, sotto voice of the man called out to him. Kuumba was slightly unsure who the voice belonged to, but he assumed, "Hey is this-?" Before Kuumba finished his sentence, the voice interrupted, "Jaylen!" Then Jaylen chuckled and continued, "I made it out, Mr. Douglas!" Kuumba's eyes clouded with tears, his lips stretched to form a slight smile, but he was speechless. "Hello, Mr. Douglas. You still there?" Jaylen persisted.

Kuumba snapped back to reality then cleared his throat and exclaimed, "Jaylen, that's great news. When did they release you?" "This morning, I'm still in the clothes they gave me." Jaylen expressed and chuckled again. Kuumba did not believe it. The prayers he offered to God every morning worked. He let out a breathy laugh and drank his coffee. "So, where are you now?" Kuumba asked. "Well, I ain't got no place to go, so the parole officer dropped me off at a homeless shelter downtown. So that's where I'm at." Jaylen replied. Kuumba sat in his car silently, phone to his ear with one hand on the steering wheel, smiling. "Hey Jaylen, how would you feel if I came to pick you up and took you to my place or to eat?"

He answered, "That would be great, Mr. Douglas. I'd appreciate that." Before Jaylen hung up, Kuumba was on the highway heading downtown. He was stuck in traffic for a while but sped through the cars when traffic cleared until he reached Jaylen. Jaylen stood outside the shelter, smoking a cigarette wearing khaki pants and a black fleece shirt. He flicked his cigarette and climbed in once Kuumba arrived. Before Jaylen put his second foot in, he was asked, "Where the hell you get the cigarette from?" as the smell of American spirit cigarettes permeated the car. Kuumba cleared his throat, squinted his eyes, and opened all the car doors for the smell to leave the vehicle. Jaylen prayed, "My bad, Mr. Douglas. I needed one, and one of the men that stayed here gave me one when I asked." A smile persisted on Kuumba's face then he drove off and drove Jaylen to get some food and clothes.

Part 3

When Jaylen was released from prison, he would stay in the homeless shelter with his ankle monitor while Kuumba helped him find a job. Kuumba would pick him up in the morning, or midday, to take him to his house or out to explore the city. One day, while Kuumba was working in his office, he received a call from his son. He hesitated to pick it up at first but eventually did. "Daddy, Daddy, Daddy!" Zaire hollered. "I'm here, son. What's going on?" "You need to come home. Mama was just taken to the hospital by an ambulance."

"Hospital! What happened?" Kuumba hollered. "I don't know, but she was shaking uncontrollably in her room. I ain't know what to do, so I called the ambulance for her. They about to take her right now!"

"Alright, alright. Calm down, son!" Kuumba tried calming his son, though he was anxious himself. "Where your brother and sister at?" he asked.

"They at their after-school program," Zaire replied with a cracked voice.

"Alright, which hospital are they taking her to?" Kuumba asked. "They told me they were taking her to St. Theresa Specialty Hospital."

"Alright, you go on with her! I'll be coming soon," Kuumba packed his things and rushed to the hospital. Kuumba called Raphial to pick up his kids from the after-school program. As he was leaving the premises, Jaylen walked towards him and shouted, "Mr. Douglas!" Jaylen called a couple of times, but Kuumba's mind wasn't there. Kuumba passed Jaylen as if he did not see him.

Jaylen hollered louder, and Kuumba finally acknowledged him ,"Oh Jaylen, hey! Listen, I can't meet with you today. My wife got taken to the hospital. I gotta go see her." Kuumba's unsteady voice quivered, and Jaylen heard him stuttering as he closed his eyes to concentrate on his thoughts. "Aight, Mr. Douglas. You sound pretty bad. I wanted to see you bout something, but it can wait tho." Kuumba nodded and walked away. "Hey, Mr. Douglas, do you mind if I go with you, ya know, for support? I mean, you supported me enough. Now, I wanna do the same."

Kuumba nodded, shook his head without giving it a second thought. His thoughts imagined that Niah lost sense of reality. Jaylen climbed into the passenger's seat and buckled up as Kuumba pulled off urgently. Kuumba sped through the highway, and Jaylen looked at him to signal that he was driving too fast and making him uneasy, but Kuumba drove through red lights and stop signs recklessly. He sped until he arrived at the hospital. Then rushed into the hospital building and spoke with the receptionist who directed him to the room Niah was in. When he made it to the room he hurried to her bed, "Hey baby, are you okay? I love you!" Then kissed her forehead and caressed her hands, and pleaded, "I'm here, baby. Whatever you need, I'm here." Kuumba kept uttering and consoling Niah and Zaire.

Shortly after, the doctor walked in with the report and Kuumba bombarded him by saying, "Doctor, my name is Kuumba Douglas, and I'm Niah's husband. How's my wife? Is she alright? What happened to her? I ain't neva seen her like this." He politely took a step back and muttered, "She's fine, Mr. Douglas." Once Kuumba conceded, the doctor walked toward Niah and began checking her out. After doing a few brief tests the doctor looked at Kuumba and implored, "Mr. Douglas, your wife is doing well. She can go home today. She had a seizure and what we call PNES."

"What's a PNES?" Kuumba asked. "Well, PNES are attacks that look like epileptic seizures but are not. They are triggered by psychological factors or a flash of traumatic events. PNES are a manifestation of psychological distress triggered by trauma. So people with PNES experience generalized convulsions, which includes falling and shaking."

"Are you saying my wife has epilepsy?" Kuumba interjected. Jaylen watched Kuumba's frantic behavior. He had never seen Kuumba in that state. Kuumba was always well put together and courageous, with no hint of fear. He saw the depressive look on Niah, the dried lips, and the colorless face. Kuumba always described Niah as strong to Jaylen, but Jaylen did not see that strength Kuumba described. She sure ain't look strong, Jaylen thought, as he kept looking at Niah and back at Kuumba. Jaylen sensed her presence, and he felt connected to Niah, although he did not know why.

"No, it's not epilepsy, its non-epileptic seizures. She suffers from recurrent depression and PTSD because of some childhood trauma she may have experienced. She might have faced subsequent abandonment, loss, abuse, or neglect. These phenomena, if not addressed early on, can develop seizure-like episodes, and that is what your wife experiences." The doctor continued.

Kuumba recalled the nights Niah would roll over in their baby's room. Kuumba would advise her to give that room to Zaire or Titus because the room held such negative memories, but Niah would refuse. Niah still believed her last-born baby was alive. Kuumba remembered Niah's shaking and convulsions, and he would rock her until they ceased. The doctor adjusted his glasses and continued, "There is no abnormal brain activity. When we checked on the video-EEG, we found the symptoms and signs of non-epileptic seizures. So we believe Niah has recurrent depression, perhaps even Dysthymia and PTSD."

"What is Dysthymia?" Kuumba asked. "Well, it's persistent depressive disorder, which is a long-term, chronic form of depression. This depression makes you lose interest in normal daily activities, feel hopeless, lack productivity, and develop low self-esteem. Now, Dysthymia or PDD can be caused by biological differences, brain chemistry, inherited traits, simple life events, or life traumas." Kuumba knew it was the trauma Niah experienced as a child and the trauma of losing their last pregnancy. Kuumba made sure Niah was asleep then whispered, "Ugh, doctor. I've been tryna get her to seek some help, but she doesn't want any."

"It's normal for her. She doesn't think she needs help, but without help, this will only worsen." The doctor emphasized. "So, how can we help her? Will she be okay?" Kuumba asked. "She will be fine. I will recommend some medication such as SSRIs or antidepressants. Plus, Psychotherapy will also work. Psychotherapy is treating depression by talking about your condition and issues with a mental health professional. She could do a few types of therapy like psychological counseling, or cognitive-behavioral therapies. That will help her."

Kuumba could not wrap his mind around his wife having depression. He couldn't understand it and had only heard about depression from afar, but now it was in his home. He took a deep breath and asked, "So, what do I do, doctor, for the PNES and the PDD?" The doctor answered, "Well, for both the PNES and the PDD, I recommend cognitive-behavioral therapy. PNES is something someone develops for harm-avoidance or self-protection because of perceived threats. Now, I suggest you go to a neurologist. However, if you need treatment, I'll recommend seeing a psychiatrist or counselor. The neurologist will further assist you, but for now, you can take your wife home." The doctor handed Kuumba a paper with recommended medications for her PDD, and they drove back home.

Jaylen studied the scene from start to finish. Kuumba loved Niah, and Jaylen saw it. He ain't never seen that type of love that Niah and Kuumba shared. When they arrived home, Jaylen drifted to open the door, while Kuumba held Niah's hand to walk her inside, and Zaire watched from behind holding Niah's bag. Kuumba took Niah to their bedroom, and Zaire trudged up the stairs to his room. Kuumba helped lay Niah onto their bed, and Niah grunted. Kuumba asked, "You okay, baby?" She nodded, and he sneered, "Alright, but you gotta rest like the doctor said. Niah ignored the reinforcement for rest and began grilling Kuumba about where the kids were and other household responsibilities. Her husband assured her everything was ok, then kissed her lips and professed his love for her.

Kuumba clomped downstairs and saw Zaire speaking with Jaylen. "Oh word," Jaylen replied to Zaire. Kuumba did not know the conversation but stood amid the staircase to listen.

"Yeah, I ain't all that bad with basketball, but I can show you," Zaire hollered. "Who's your favorite basketball player?" Jaylen asked. "Man, Kobe all the way. The greatest basketball player of our time. Can't nobody beat Kobe Bryant." Zaire replied. "That's for sure!" Jaylen snapped and nodded his head. Kuumba joined their conversation and approved their conclusion. "Y'all got it right." "Oh word, Mr. Douglas," Jaylen nagged with a lopsided smile.

After a few more minutes of talking basketball, Kuumba urged, "So, I gotta go pick up Titus and Ujamaa at Raphial's house. Who wanna come?" "I'll come!" Jaylen answered, then Zaire reluctantly decided to join. Zaire wanted to stay in his room and play his guitar, but he obliged because Kuumba gave him an unflinching stare. They took off, and Niah stood by the window glancing at them.

When they arrived at Raphial's house, the kids ran to the car, and Raphial conversed with Kuumba. They spoke for a while and then said their goodbyes. Once they all left, Kuumba asked his kids so that he could know their state of mind, "How are y'all doin?"

"It was good. We learned about fractions and read some books." Ujamaa exclaimed.

"What about you, Titus?" Kuumba continued. "It was alright. It could have been better. Why did you just come to pick us up daddy?" Titus inquired, as his compelling hazel brown eyes gazed at his father in the rearview mirror. "I had some stuff to take care of, and I had to take mama to the hospital," he answered. "Mama to the hospital?

What happened?" Ujamaa asked. Once they pulled up to the house he pressed on, "She wasn't feeling well." The kids raced into the house and bumped into Zaire. "Hey, watch where y'all goin!" he yelled. Titus waved his hands and yelled, "Shut up!" Kuumba asked both of them to clean up and help prepare dinner.

Jaylen followed Kuumba into the house and sat by the dining room table. Kuumba went into his bedroom and spotted Niah sleeping. He kissed her, "Baby, we back. I'mma make us some food. You want anything?"

Niah stretched, leached out of her blankets and leaned in as if she expected to be buried in Kuumba's aroma, "I'm fine. I just need some spicy soup. How are the kids?"

"They are good. I'll make you some." Before Kuumba finished his statement, Ujamaa and Titus came running into the room to Niah. "Mama!" Ujamaa climbed on the bed, and half hugged her mother. Titus approached the side of the bed interrogating her mother, "Mama, you okay?" Niah closed her eyes, gasped for air, still inhaling her husband's aroma to calm her. "Yah baby, I just need some rest." Then Kuumba interrupted, "Alright, y'all heard yo mama. Go on downstairs, let her rest." Kuumba interrupted.

Titus and Ujamaa ran downstairs to where Zaire and Jaylen were. Kuumba headed to the kitchen and started cooking. Jaylen spoke with the kids, and Zaire asked him questions. "Hmm, Zaire, come help me make dinner." Kuumba summoned Zaire because he realized he was asking Jaylen too many questions.

"But Daddy!" Zaire threw his hands high and rolled his eyes. "But nothin. Come help, so cooking can go faster." Zaire plodded to the kitchen to help his daddy make dinner. Jaylen asked, "How can I help Mr. Douglas?" He wanted to return the favor to Kuumba for his constant love and support. Kuumba directed Jaylen, and they cooked dinner together, while Titus watched cartoons, and Ujamaa went back upstairs to tend to her mama.

When they finished cooking, Kuumba took some soup to Niah, and Ujamaa offered to feed her mama. Zaire, Titus, and Jaylen gathered around the dining room table and waited for Kuumba. The food was greasy, and the juicy aroma from the food hugged the kids. Once the head of the household joined the table he cleared his throat,, "Zaire, please bless the food." When Zaire finished praying, they dug into their food, but it did not feel the same without Niah sitting at the table. Kuumba kept checking up the stairs every other second to see if Niah would come downstairs to join them. After dinner, the children cleaned the table and dishes then veered to their mama's room. Jaylen remained in the living room area with Kuumba. "I hope Mrs. Douglas will be aight." Jaylen looked at Kuumba uneasily and responded, "Yeah, Jaylen, me too." "I know she will, Mr. Douglas. I know she will cause she got you and I know you ain't gonna let nothin' bad happen to her. She was lucky to have you," Jaylen continued. The mentor and mentee talked until midnight. Kuumba offered to let Jaylen stay the night in their home instead of going to the homeless shelter. "Yeah, that would be cool, but you gotta let em know cause them parole officers will come looking for me at the shelter if I'm not there." Jaylen seemed excited, yet nervous.

Kuumba assured that he would call the shelter first thing in the morning and gave him a blanket and a pillow to sleep on the living room sofa. "Daddy, Jaylen can come stay in my room if he wants?"

Zaire offered. Jaylen smiled and laid on his back then responded, "Nah, I'm good right here. Thanks, though."

The kids quickly fell asleep, and Kuumba rushed to Niah's side to comfort her until they both fell asleep. In the morning, the sunlight trickled through the sheer white curtains in the master bedroom. She woke up, sat on the edge of her bed, eyes hollowed and engrossed by bags under her eyes as if she did not sleep. She sighed and searched for energy to combat her exhaustion. She dragged her feet to the kitchen to make breakfast, and the kids wrapped their arms around her. Jaylen woke up to the gleeful sound of love which was foreign to him. He walked to the kitchen but stood far from everyone. Niah turned to face Jaylen with a shrewd look. "You must be Jaylen!" Niah exclaimed.

With a cracked bashful smile Jaylen returned the warm greetings Niah gave to him. "You must be Mrs. Douglas." Jaylen boasted, knowing that he's been waiting to meet with her.

Niah looked at him and summoned him to sit down alongside the kids for breakfast. She served them breakfast while Kuumba walked down the stairs wearing a suit and fixing his tie. He kissed Niah as soon as he entered the kitchen then sat down with everyone. They enjoyed breakfast and prattled until Kuumba took the kids to school. Niah stayed home with Jaylen.

Jaylen asked to help around the house, the backyard, and with anything he could. "Mrs. Douglas, I hope you gettin' better. I saw how Mr. Douglas was freakin' out yesterday, speeding' through the highway, and nearly had a heart attack to come see you."

"I'm fine, Jaylen. Thank you. I just had a lot of convulsions. That's all." Jaylen nodded, gazed around the house admiring the decor and the wooden floors, "You have a pleasant home here, Mrs Douglas. "She replied, ". I'm glad you like it. I try to make it as homely as possible." There was a pause, and Jaylen yelped "I heard a lot of excellent things about you from Mr. Douglas. He always brings your name up. It seems like we experienced the same thing."

Niah grabbed a cup of coffee and came to join him at the dining table. She looked at him, placed both her hands on her coffee mug, and began asking Jaylen a series of questions. She was unsure why she felt connected to him, but she continued to dig deeper. "So Jaylen, tell me about yourself, your family. Where are they at?" Niah asked. "To be honest, Mrs. Douglas, I don't know. I ain't from here. I was born and raised in South Carolina and lived with my mama and my daddy, but he never really came home much. He was always out. Then, one day while he was in the streets hustling, they shot him dead cold like an animal." Jaylen paused. "I ain't never forget that day. I mean, he was never there for me, but it was good to know he was alive. When he passed, all hell broke loose. My mama went crazy. She was pregnant at the time and couldn't support us. My mama couldn't get a word out for several days.

Niah saw Jaylen sinking deep into his darkest thoughts. "After a while, my mama found somebody else. He was good to her. He took care of her, loved her, cared for her, and cared for me. He taught me how to do things, become a man, and restore peace in the house. Sometimes he drank and raised his voice at my mama, but he did take care of her. He was the man of the house. Sometimes he left for days at a time, but my mama never questioned it. She loved his sanctuary."

51

Jaylen paused, and watched Niah's hand tracing the brims of her coffee mug.

"So how did you end up here, in jail, and why didn't you stay with your mama and step daddy." Niah implored. "To be honest, Mrs. Douglas, I don't know what got into me. I started following in my daddy's footsteps, got caught up with the wrong crowd, and started selling drugs, stealing, and breaking the law. The first time I got arrested, my step daddy came to bail me out and gave me some money. Even though he would beat me sometimes, he's still the best daddy I ever had. "He wasn't no Mr. Douglas," Jaylen chuckled. "But he was a suitable replacement for my real daddy," Jaylen replied.

Niah flashed a warm smile and muttered, "Well, I'm glad someone came to replace your daddy." "Yeah, but he passed away while I was doing time. When I got out, they told me he died in his sleep." Jaylen snarled. "Then, they wouldn't even let me attend the funeral. He taught me a lot. His death made my mama cry for years. She ain't never been the same. Unfortunately, I haven't seen her in ten years, so I don't know if she's alive or not. I don't even know what my little sister looks like and that hurts me every day, Mrs. Douglas."

Niah looked at Jaylen with a passionate look. "I guess we ain't no different, Jaylen. I'm sorry about that, and I'm glad you found a daddy in your life. My daddy left me. He left a year after my mama developed breast cancer. My mama was in and out of the hospital. I had to pay my mama's medical bills and take care of my mama, but she passed away." Niah cried.

"I'm sorry for your loss, Mrs. Douglas. I hope you heal from it. I see you haven't healed." Jaylen paused and caught Niah's eyes wide open as if she had seen a ghost. Niah looked at the small boy, teaching her a thing or two. Jaylen smirked, "If I had a daddy like Mr. Douglas, I wouldn't be here. I envy Zaire and Titus. They have a noble father." He chuckled, then pulled out a necklace around his chest and caressed the brim of the necklace. "I wanted to get his name tattooed on my chest, but I never had the courage to do it."

"What was your daddy's name?" Niah asked. Jaylen responded, "My daddy's name was Darrell Cleveland." Niah pried, "What was your step daddy's name?" He answered, "Hakim McClananan Wilburn." Niah paused, eyes widened. She whispered, "Hakim? Hakim? Hakim?" The name rang a bell. She couldn't recall what about the name rang a bell.

Hakim. Niah continued to ponder on that name. She's heard it before, perhaps in her dreams or a conversation in church.

Jaylen tried interrupting her thoughts to ask if she was okay. But Niah felt trapped in a memory she did not seem to recognize. "Sorry it's just that, that name rings a bell. I don't know where I heard the name, but it sounds familiar."

Niah and Jaylen pondered for a moment, until Jaylen proposed that she might have met a man with that name. Under her breath Niah whispered softly "No."

The name seemed distant yet close. She continued to frisk her mental library for answers. Hakim was just not another name. Niah's mom was named Maya Wilburn. But she still couldn't understand why Hakim felt like her broken sanctuary, so she brushed it aside, and they continued talking.

Jaylen asked, "Well, what is your daddy's name?" Niah reflected and answered, "He was a grown-ass man calling himself Husky. That wasn't his actual name, but everybody called him that, even his mama." It felt like a long time since she dug the memory of her father from her heart. It seemed as if her daddy was dead to her, even in her memory.

Niah's eyes turned away from Jaylen while she chuckled. She felt like she had to venture in the leaden path of her childhood memories to speak on her father. After Jaylen saw the troubled look on her face, he implored, "Why did they call him that, Mrs. D?"

She responded, "When he was younger he had a husky. That dog was his best friend. My mama told me about that. He was always with that dog anywhere he was. He was a lonely child, and his dog kept him out of trouble until the dog passed. My mama told me he adopted the name Husky to honor his best friend for life, but he forgot to honor himself."

"Damn, that's sad. I'm sorry about your father," Jaylen offered. Niah straightened and attempted to chuckle, "Nah, Jaylen, don't be. If I could disown him, I would. He was never a father. He was just a boy who impregnated a woman three times. Not a man to take care of his household."

"Aight, I'm sorry you experienced that, Mrs. D. I guess we ain't no different," Jaylen sneered as he cracked his knuckles. Niah agreed, but the question about her father's real name haunted her. "What would you like to eat, Jaylen?" Niah tried to change the subject of the conversation. "Well, I'll eat just about anything, Mrs. Douglas. Mr. Douglas told me you make the best gumbo!" Jaylen chucked and nibbled on his bottom lip as a smile plastered across Niah's face.

She chittered, "My mama taught me how to make gumbo before she died. She used to throw down in the kitchen," they shared a priceless laugh and continued, "She was a woman that would cook every Sunday, and my church would all come eat at our place." Jaylen added in, "I grew up in church too. I didn't used to believe in God, but that all changed when I was in prison. While behind bars, I learned so much about life and God. I was going insane and needed something to hold on to, and there was a priest who came talking about God and gave us mini-bibles. At first, I did not believe what I read, but when I prayed, everything in my life changed, including my character, soul, and mind."

After Jaylen finished eating, he then left before Kuumba returned home. Niah felt a sense of healing while talking and thinking about her father. She forgot he existed, and it felt good, so it took her a while to pull the memories of his real name. The day was dull, yet everlasting. She sat outside and wished it passed by faster, but each hour seemed longer than the next.

She loved the weather in Kenner, Louisiana, which is located on the outskirts of New Orleans. Niah felt that the warm weather, cajun food, French and Spanish influence was second to none. She loved to travel through the bayou to see the alligators. Although she did not like the swamps, she cherished her state. Over the next couple of days, Jaylen came by the house to eat, clean, and converse with Niah. Niah felt deeply connected to Jaylen, but she was unsure why. Kuumba helped Jaylen get a job at Home Depot. When Jaylen began working, he started coming by less often and Kuumba missed his presence.

One day Niah went through her old pictures, her mama's bible, and read all the letters her mama ever wrote for her. An image stuck out to her. It was a family picture of when she was young. She stood next to her brother. Her mama sat on a gray couch, hugging her, and her daddy sat next to her mama. They looked like a happy family and all of them had smiles. It was the opposite of the image that stuck out in her mind when she typically thought about her family. Niah's smile turned upside down once she stared at her father, so she turned the picture over. On the back of the photograph, her mama wrote in cursive,

"Annie McClannan Wilburn, Stevie McClannan Wilburn, Niah McClannan Wilburn, Maya McClannan Wilburn, and Hakim McClannan Wilburn. My happy and lovely family. I love y'all. Love Mama."

Her eyes widened, lips turned dry, and she dropped the photo. Hakim McClannan Wilburn was her father's name. Her stomach growled and her face cracked, then she whispered, "Hakim? Niah Wilburn..." Jaylen knocked as she began processing everything.

Once he entered, Jaylen asked if everything was ok. Niah was in awe, puzzled, and unsure. Niah did not want to answer. Jaylen rushed to her side then picked up the picture that sent Niah into a tailspin. She looked up, then they locked eyes,, "Oh, that's my step-daddy, Hakim!" Then pulled out the necklace he wore with a picture of Hakim and him and showed it to Niah.

Both of their hearts hit the floor when they realized Jaylen's stepdaddy was Niah's biological daddy. Jaylen looked at Niah with remorse, he felt that Niah's plight was his fault. "Damn, Mrs. Douglas, I'm sorry! I didn't know he had a family. He never mentioned that to us. I ain't mean to take your daddy away from you."

So, Jaylen and his mama were the reason daddy was never home. I ain't never had a daddy's love because he stole it from me, Niah thought. Jaylen got up after seeing that he couldn't get through to her.

Niah grabbed her PDD medication and swallowed them dry. Then she sat on the toilet seat as her body trembled. She couldn't digest the unthinkable news.

Once Kuumba returned home he spotted a note on the table. It read, "Dear Mr. and Mrs. Douglas, I ain't neva wanna cause trouble. Imma leave y'all since I ain't wanna hurt nobody. Thanks for your love. Peace."

Kuumba searched around the house, then found Niah trembling on the toilet seat. "Hey Niah, you okay, baby? Everything alright? Jaylen left a notice." She hesitated and answered, "Yeah, I'm fine," but Kuumba did not believe her answer. He babbled, "Well, I met with a psychotherapist, and I think she will be very helpful. Her name is Dr. Moore Felicia. I told her about your case, and she wants to help you." I really think you should see her baby. You need healing. You need to talk to a professional. I know you will get better when you do." Niah took heed to the love and concern her husband showed and agreed to go beyond her will.

Days passed, and Niah started her psychotherapy. Kuumba tried to locate Jaylen, but to no avail. The shelter Jaylen stayed at did not disclose any information on his whereabouts. Niah recovered, opened up, and spoke about her experiences and past, but still couldn't come to grips with the situation with her father and Jaylen. He died without her knowing. He was more of a father to Jaylen than he ever was to her. It didn't sit well with her that he helped his mistress, while his wife died in the hospital. She didn't know how to feel, but knew it wasn't right to blame Jaylen for her father's wrongs. Niah kept the situation from her husband until several months after it occurred.

She opened up about it after a severe nightmare. Once Niah frantically jumped out of her sleep she asked, "Have you found any information on Jaylen?"

"No. I don't know where he is. He might have left the shelter. I can't seem to find or get a hold of him." Niah paused, then pleaded, "Baby, the day he left here, I found out that his step-daddy was my real daddy. He left my mama for Jaylen's mama. He was more of a father to him than me." Niah felt paralyzed reliving that moment she discovered that Jaylen was fathered by her father more than she was.

Kuumba didn't know what to think. For a moment, he thought she made this up to cover up for him getting arrested again.

She continued, "I ain't never forgetting what that man did to my mama. He left her to die while he went to another woman. He spit and beat me while he protected another baby. What kind of man is that?" Kuumba saw anger, hurt, rage, and dismay in her eyes. "Niah, I know you are hurt. I get that. I understand you've gone through so much. I'm sorry, baby. No child should go through that. He was no man, but baby, if you ain't gonna forgive your daddy and forgive your past, you ain't gon' heal. You've hanged yourself with the ropes of hurt and your daddy's past. If you keep focusing so much on the past, you gonna miss the beauty of the present and future. You gotta learn to forgive. Jaylen ain't to blame. He was runnin and lonely, just like you. He needed love, just like you. You and him ain't no different. It ain't his fault that man came into his life. It's wrong of your daddy to leave you for another child, but don't punish Jaylen for it, baby, please. He was tryna survive just like you."

She barked back, "What do you mean he was tryna survive? He did survive. He had his own daddy and mama. Why does it gotta be my daddy? It's not fair," Niah vented. While she cried in Kuumba's comforting arms she wished to watch her daddy drown or die a slow, painful death. Then she wondered, what kind of child wishes their father to die a slow and painful death. Niah continued to ponder, but she remembered Kuumba's words. Jaylen was lonely, just like her and ended up in a harsh situation as well. Her father's presence in Jaylen's life didn't keep him out of jail. Though Jaylen was in a physical prison, she became mentally institutionalized. Jaylen's trauma wasn't to be taken lightly.

While Kuumba talked with her, she felt guilty that Jaylen might have disappeared because of her. All Jaylen needed was love but received trauma. She thought, ain't that what I needed too? I ain't never meant to hurt him. Sometimes, we focus so much on our own trauma that we forget other folks got trauma too.

Kuumba didn't sleep the following days. He contacted every shelter in the city to find him, but they did not help. Kuumba intensified his prayers that Jalen was not in jail.

Niah went to her therapy sessions. Niah's therapist urged her to let go, forgive, and amend her brokenness, but another nightmare came to Niah's mind. She told the therapist, "Jaylen ran because of me. I ain't never forgivin' myself if that boy goes back to prison. Jaylen ain't no different from me. I ain't got no family, but that doesn't mean Jaylen shouldn't have one. We shared the same daddy. Though not blood, I'm his closest of kin." After embracing Jaylen and opening up to the therapist, she began feeling a sense of healing.

Several weeks passed without anyone hearing from Jaylen. One evening, while Kuumba and Niah sat on their brown couch, cuddling and watching the local news, a reporter claimed, "A 28-year old black male named, Jaylen Montgomery, was shot yesterday at Julia Train Station as he was a bystander of an altercation between two teens. There have been no updates on his condition, but authorities stated he was shot in the arm." Kuumba and Niah's hearts were on the floor while they stared at Jaylen's picture on the television screen. Kuumba drowned in defeat and Niah sulked in guilt. They cried and hugged each other until they gained enough strength to rush out the house. Kuumba called Jaylen's phone eight times before he answered, "Yo, Mr. Douglas."

"Hey, Jaylen! Are you okay, son? Where are you?" Kuumba's voice cracked as he sped through the night. Jaylen responded, "Yeah, I'm gettin better. I'm at the New Orleans East Hospital." Each word he spoke carried a heaviness as if he was running out of breath. Kuumba shouted, "Okay, hold tight, we're hurrying your way!"

Jaylen felt a love he couldn't fathom. They loved him as if he was their son, and Jaylen couldn't process it. Kuumba drove into the hospital's parking lot, and they rushed inside. When they arrived, the receptionist took them to Jaylen's room. Once they entered, he whimpered, "Hey, Mr. Douglas, Mrs. Douglas. Y'all made it." With a cracking but comforting voice, Niah approached Jaylen, "We sure did. How are you doing?"

"I'm doin good. Getting better. My arm hurts though." Jaylen chuckled, and his lips formed a lopsided grin, but Niah knew it was forced. "We're glad you're okay." Kuumba held Niah's hands as they both looked at Jaylen. The room was dim and silent except for the medical machines humming.

Jaylen broke the silence and said , "Mrs. Douglas, I am sorry," while maintaining a cold, unflinching stare. "For what, Jaylen?" Niah asked. Jaylen paused, licked his lips, and turned his face to the side, then answered, "I ain't never meant to take your daddy away from you." Niah's face felt paralyzed. She was turning hot, and her lips exhibited oncoming dryness. He continued, "I ain't never meant to do that to you or anybody. He ain't never told us about having no family or kids. When he left for a few days and returned, he told us he went on business trips."

She gently touched his wounded arm, and felt a gush of blood rushing through his veins. "It wasn't your fault. Never was, and never will be. He never loved us anyway, so I stopped loving him too." Jaylen responded, "If I'd known he did that to you, I wouldn't have accepted him into my life. He left y'all like my daddy left me. I'm really sorry." Jaylen's knees felt weak as he grunted and his hand fisted. Niah held Jaylen's hand, and it slowly softened. She responded, "I know, Jaylen. I'm sorry too. Don't blame yourself." Jaylen grinned and pulled out his hand to fist bump Niah. They all laughed, and Kuumba joined them.

"But there is one thing our daddy did right," Niah muttered. Jaylen widened her eyes and raised her elbows. Niah chuckled. "Excuse my language, but that bitch pulled us together. If he ain't did what he did, I wouldn't have known I had an amazing little brotha out there. You've become a glowing part of my life. Even though we had less than desirable lives, we got each other now." Niah's almond eyes gazed at Jaylen, as he formulated a priceless smile.

They all stayed in the room for a little while, Jaylen pulled himself onto the bed to rest, and Niah huddled closer to Kuumba. He looked deep into her eyes and said, "You are glowin, baby. Baby, I'mma work for the legacy of that boy." "Me too," she replied, while still watching Jaylen sleep.

Before leaving, Niah paused, breathing in the hope that she felt lingered in the room, "My brother, I love you. I always will. I always got your back. I'mma work to build with you a good legacy." This was what Niah needed. An untimely forgiveness, that released her from her burdened load.

The untimely forgiveness brought an exodus for Niah which she couldn't understand. Niah finally forgave her father because of Jaylen. She thought of her husband's love, sons' laughter, her daughter's beauty, and thanked God for it all. Niah remembered her mama's bible and faith, and knew God existed. Jaylen was God-sent. She promised to protect and help her little brother. Being with her husband, her kids, and Jaylen became bigger than her daddy's mistake and the pain of losing her mama and her last-born. Therefore, each day she tried a little harder to improve herself for Kuumba, Ujamaa, Titus Zaire... and for her little brother, Jaylen.

Lumiere Bukasa

KANGA MOTEMA (CLOSED HEART)
LINGALA LANGUAGE

Part 1

Kaku, where does the sun go when it disappears ?" Furaha asked. Kaku looked to the sky as if the answer was hiding in the clouds and answered, "I don't know, but I know God hides it for the next day and replaces it with the moon and stars." "Why would God do that?" Furaha asked, puzzled at Kaku's statement. "I guess to show the sun that its glory has an end, just like everything else." Kaku paused, gazed at Furaha, and continued, "One day, when God created the earth, he watched everything move in its glory. He created the sun and the moon, but as he watched the sun, he saw the pride and boasting of the sun before the stars and moon that laid behind the sun. He would say, I am the great light, I shine bright, I bring the harvest and everything good. By the shine of my light, kids play, mothers dry their clothes, and water is warmed. God watched the boasting of the sun for days until one day he decided to give the sun seven hours to shine and leave space for the moon to be glorified in the night. God humbles those who glorify themselves and glorifies those who are humbled."

Furaha loved stories. She loved folktales. She loved it all. Her life consisted of stories and revolved around them. She skipped home, remembering this tale while looking at the sunset. It was beautiful. Even when its glory came to an end, it was still beautiful. A freshly picked cockatoo flower served as the cherry on the top of a magical evening.

When Furaha entered the compound, she peered at the veranda, spotting figures whose faces were hidden under the dusk evening. "There once was a woman who fell asleep during a preacher 's sermon. She woke up at the rumbling voice of the preacher roaring, 'Stand up.' The woman woke up puzzled." Kaku's voice was quiet as she spoke, yet powerful. Furaha treaded to where her cousins and family perched, heeding to Kaku's nightly tales. They all cohesively sat around the charcoal brazier and soaking in the aroma of the pondu. The pondu seethed in the pot, beating the top of the pan cover. Maman Beya rose from her spot, dis-attached her maputa, and then wrapped it around her chest tighter. She grabbed the stirring spoon, opened the pot of pondu, and stirred it until she felt it was good. After she finished stirring the pondu, she took the stirring spoon, placed the residue on her palm, and tasted the soup. She confidently nodded her head, covered the pot, and placed the spoon in a bowl of water.

Maman Beya sat back down and continued to listen to Kaku's tale. "When the preacher man yelled, 'Stand up,' the woman woke up from her nap and stood up in obedience to the preacher's words. As she was standing, she looked around the church and noticed that she was the only one standing. She then noticed that every eye was focused on her. Confused, she looked at her husband sitting next to her, and he looked back at her in the same manner. The preacher man looked at her and shouted, "Thank you for your courage to stand up. We will pray to God for you." He then shouted, "Does anyone else care to join her in the presence of God?" The preacher man cleared his throat then enlightened her on the reason for her standing. He said, "I asked you to stand if you committed adultery and cannot stop cheating on your partner. I asked this so we can pray for you."

Everyone burst into laughter as if it was their first time listening to Kaku's tale.

They shared laughs, and Furaha turned to her cousin Penda and bumped her shoulder as they laughed concurrently. Kaku leaned back in her chair with a simper, exposing her pearly white teeth and the dimple on her cheek. "Kaku, please tell us another tale." Penda bellowed and gawked at grandmother.

"Hapana. Ni wakati wa kula chakula." Kaku pointed at the pot of fufu and the pot of Ndagala. "Penda, go and fetch water for us to wash our hands." Maman Ngondu summoned her daughter Penda. Penda grabbed a plastic container and sprinted to the other side of the house to fetch water from the green water tank. She climbed on a stone to reach the brim of the water tank and scooped enough to fill the container.

Penda rushed back to the veranda while her eyes shone with mirth. She sat down on the veranda floor, crossed her feet, dipped her plump hands into the water, then felt knuckles grazing across her head. Penda felt her sweltering blood rush through her veins, paralyzing her and dousing her appetite, even though the pondu and ndakala seemed mouthwatering. "Don't ever wash your hands before your elders!" Maman Ngondu rolled her eyes and yelled at Penda. She snatched the container, then passed it to one person, who passed it to another within the circle until it reached Nkoko, Maman Ngondu's father, and Furaha's grandfather. Nkoko took the container, dipped his hands, then passed it to Kaku, who washed her hands and passed it to another, until everyone washed their hands.

Then Maman Ngondu took the fufu and passed it to Nkoko, who grabbed some ndakala. They sat in silence, eating in mere concentration as if it was the last supper. They ate that day and knew food wasn't guaranteed tomorrow. After supper, all the women carried the plates, cleared the veranda, and the men stood, stretched, and rubbed their bellies to express fullness. The women cleaned the dishes and poured water on the container while the grandparents strolled to their bedroom. They took a lamp near their bedroom door, lit a match, and closed their door. All the men of the house did the same, while the women stayed and cleaned the compound before going to sleep. Once finished, they gazed at all the young sons laying around the tile floor like sardines in a can. The room felt muggy and damp as the fan roared in the background. Some of the sons snored like hibernating bears. The women pushed them aside to make room for more bodies. Each woman found a place to lay. Furaha climbed on the bed that miraculously held six bodies. Legs were innocently entangled with other people's faces on the mattress. It was an uncomfortable room, filled with memories as sweet as bitter leaves.

The night held an unusual aroma of deceit and a flush of stories Kaku told earlier. Furaha couldn't sleep. Her mind aimlessly wondered, and her eyes blankly stared at intrinsic details of the room. She gazed at the window and caught a glimpse of a figure who appeared to be a man soliciting by the window and seeking entrance into the house. A deluge of fear overwhelmed Furaha, and the thought of this figure ailed her ability to sleep.

Furaha felt relieved when she opened her eyes the following morning. Making it through the night felt like an accomplishment. She heard Kaku humming and cleaning the veranda. Kaku was always the first person to wake up. Routinely she woke up before sunrise and prepared herself before anyone else.

Furaha rose from the bed and walked to the door. Once she opened the door, a refreshing breeze enlarged her pores. She smiled at Kaku. "Betu'abu," Furaha greeted her grandmother. "Betu," her grandmother replied and led Furaha to the latrine. When she finished using the latrine, Kaku took a bucket of water, undressed Furaha, poured cold water on her body, and began to scrub her with a loofah sponge.

Furaha's body shivered as she wrapped her arms around herself to bring warmth to her body but all failed. Kaku finished, took one of her maputas, and wiped Furaha dry. Kaku grabbed shea butter and plastered it on every inch of Furaha's body. She went into her room and grabbed Furaha's uniform that was safely hidden under her maputas. She brought it out and gave it to Furaha to wear. "You better not stain this uniform. You know you only have one. Your father has not sent money to buy you new clothes. You understand?" Kaku instructed. "Ndio," Furaha replied.

She proudly wore her torn uniform and battered shoes. "Manage, my daughter. God will bless you one day." Kaku lifted Furaha's chin. Mama Tshibelu and Maman Ngondu woke up and walked to Kaku when Furaha sprinted out of the compound for school. "Why are you spoiling her like this? Why don't you treat your other grandkids like this?" Maman Tshibelu asserted. Kaku looked at Maman Tshibelu with a smirk and responded, "Because all the other grandchildren have both their parents here. Her parents are not here. Her father sought a better life for her in a country that he does not know. She is alone here. I will care for her until her father comes for her."

"She's your favorite, Kaku, we know," Maman Tshibelu expressed and rolled her eyes. Kaku smiled and continued her morning chores. Furaha arrived at school and sat around one of the bricks encompassing a raffia palm tree, waiting for the bell to ring. Her friend, Nyota, greeted her and sat next to her. Nyota arrived with her breakfast box including two slices of bread overfilled with avocado. "You didn't bring your food?" Nyota muttered. "No, I ate at home before coming." Furaha lied to conceal her poverty as her stomach viciously growled in disagreement.

The bell rang, and Professor Tshisenga walked out of the classroom, peevishly, with a wooden clipboard. All the students silently and militantly ran to make two lines in front of the teacher. They recited the Lord's prayer before Professor Tshisenga escorted them into the classroom, rearranged the books on his desk, took a piece of chalk, and wrote *"Belgian Congo 1940s."*

When he turned back to the class, he began his roll call. "Alain," he asserted. "Present," Alain answered. He continued, "Glody." "Present," Glody stood up and exclaimed. He continued through the list until he arrived at Furaha's name. "Furaha," he asserted and dropped his clipboard on his desk. "Present," Furaha babbled. As she was about to sit down, Professor Tshisenga sharply declared, "You did not pay your school fees for this month. You cannot stay in the class. Leave now!" He emanated with anger, stared at Furaha, repeatedly stating, "Pack your stuff and leave the class right now!"

She mercifully dropped to her knees and pleaded, "Professor, Kaku will pay for me! This month has been hard on us, and we don't have money at the moment, but I will work my hardest to pay for it. Please find it in your heart to let me stay." The heart-spilling speech didn't move the Professor, and he still coldly asked her to leave.

Furaha sprinted home with bitter tears falling to the concrete with each stride. She made it back to the compound while her grandmother rested under her avocado tree, and the other women washed clothes or swept the compound with African brooms. Once Furaha arrived back several hours before her usual time, they stared at her. Kaku asked, "Furaha, why are you not in school?" Furaha paused, inhaled, and started crying again. Everyone waited for her to regain her composure, then she responded, "Professor Tshisenga kicked me out because I don't have school fees."

Kaku's reeked of disgust, and responded, "I told that man that we don't have money, and when your father sends money next month, we will pay! We will sleep without food tonight. Where will we find the money to pay for these fees?" Furaha stood silently as Kaku expressed her rage. "We are going to go see this professor." Kaku led Furaha out of the compound, and they marched back to the school.

Kaku burst into the classroom, raised her voice, and implored publicly, "Baba, why are you taking an opportunity from a child because of money? I already told you that we will pay when her father sends money!" Gasps filled the classroom, and Furaha felt the need to hide in plain sight. The class was in utter disbelief as Mr. Tshisenga, a man who intimidates, was being intimidated. Furaha stood outside in shame as Kaku exposed their household struggles. She continued, "Baba, we live each day without knowing what the next one will bring. We eat one day and don't the next. Today, there is no food to eat. We are suffering to survive and eat each meal, waiting for our death. Where will we get money to pay for her school fees? Please let her stay, at least for this month. We will pay when her father sends money. Please, baba wetu!" He complied and answered,

"Okay, mama. She can stay, but only for this month. If she does not pay by the thirteenth, which is in two weeks, she will have to unenroll from this school." "Thank you. May God bless you," Kaku uttered as she took a corner piece of her maputa and wiped her tears. Then she walked to the hallway and shouted, "Furaha, come take your place in the classroom."

The Professor continued his lecture, "Okay, we have spoken about King Leopold II of Belgium and his arrival in Congo in the 1940's. What was he doing in Congo?" Furaha answered, "Professor, King Leopold came to bring back the lost civilization of Congo." Mr. Tshisengu nodded in agreement. "Anything else?" he asked. Before another student could answer, she chimed in, "But in the process, he killed over ten million Congolese. The world saw this and stopped it because it was awful."

Mr. Tshisenga lifted his eyebrows in amusement, "Wow, great job! You could have a seat. This was a great day today, class. We will continue with history tomorrow." The bell rang, and the students remained still until the teacher dismissed the class. All the students burst out of the class in excitement except for Furaha, who sulked off the school premises.

A girl named Haya heckled, "Hey Furaha, poor girl. Living in poverty. Poverty does not look good on you."

"Poverty does not look good on anyone, Haya. No one chooses to be poor," Furaha responded and walked away. Haya followed her and taunted, "So you think you are smart now. I will beat you up right here," Haya threatened.

"I don't think I'm anything. I just want to go home, Haya. Please, leave me alone!" Furaha pressed.

Haya pushed Furaha into a muddy puddle, laughed, and peevishly spat in the puddle. Haya walked away feeling satisfied within herself. She walked away engulfed by her crowd as they praised her courage. "You think because I am poor, you can treat me anyhow? No one chooses to be poor. If God showed me that this would be my life, I'd have wished to remain unborn!" Furaha fumed, rubbing her eyes from the dirt that managed to enter her eye socket.

Once she returned home, she was bombarded with more questions than when she returned home prematurely earlier that day. "What happened? You are dirty." Maman Beya questioned. Furaha silently continued to Kaku's door and knocked. When Kaku came out, she asked questions. Furaha quickly vented about her day's nightmare. Kaku walked Furaha back to her room, then told her to look for a morsel of soap wrapped in a white plastic bag under her bed.

Once Furaha retrieved it, Kaku whispered, "I keep this for you. It's small, but I know how you play and get your uniform dirty. Go change and wash your uniform. Do not finish the soap. You will reuse it again. Do you hear me?" Furaha nodded and went to do as Kaku told her.

The sun began to set, and it was clear that this day would end without food. Kaku sat down in her rocking chair and knitted a blanket. Furaha went into the bedroom that contained the cooking pots, matches, and normally leftovers from the previous day's supper. She found nothing but a cockroach seeking food in the empty pot. Furaha grabbed a mug, poured some sugar into it, fetched water, and poured it into the mug. Then stirred the water with a spoon and drank it to quench her hunger.

Her highlight at the end of a hard day was sitting next to Kaku and listening to the humming of her grandmother's gospel song, which she turned into a lullaby. She hummed one of her favorite Tshiluba song, which went, "*Mukalenga munange, Mukalenga munange, lelu jukwimibila.*"

Although Furaha enjoyed the current moments, she exhumed the shame, resentment, and bitterness produced by an earlier encounter with Haya. It was as if Kaku felt the shift in Furaha's mood. "That energy is not welcome here, Furaha. Your heart should not hold bitterness. I know it is hard when one woman tries to destroy another woman for the sake of self-pride. We are supposed to be our sister's keeper. Let me tell you a secret. A person will only attempt to break you down when they are already broken. Rich people will always elevate others because the goodness of riches is in sharing. For what good are riches if they are not shared? What is knowledge if not given? What is the use of anything good if it's not used for good?"

Furaha sat down quietly while peeking at the veranda candle holder. "To serve another, to take care of another is to take care of oneself. We came from the same ancestors. A person abusing you is not only abusing you but the lineage of ancestors. It takes no effort to lift another sister, another black warrior. African sisters have been forced into competition and fighting as a means of feeling good about themselves. If she can't tap into the queen she is, do not lower your crown for her. Tap into the queen and warrior in you. You understand?" Kaku asserted. Furaha responded, *"Ndio."*

Silence befell the two, crickets chirped, and the spikes of fire coming from the charcoal brazier shot up in the air. Each person in the house took a corner of the compound and either told stories or played mancala games on the dirt. Kaku broke the silence and said, "Let me tell you some ancient stories of African women. Would you like that?" Furaha silently nodded with a slight grin on her face. "Do you know of Queen Aminatu?" Kaku asked. "No," Furaha muttered. Kaku matched her grin and narrated, "Oh, she was a great Hausa warrior in Nigeria. She was the eldest daughter of Queen Bakwa Turunku, who founded the Zazzau Kingdom in 1536. She ruled after her mother's death. Queen Aminatu was a great military strategist. A woman of great valor and filled with cavalry. She fought many wars and conquered most of the wars she led. She was an intelligent woman who left a mark on Nigeria and Africa." Kaku calmly paused, as if she was troubled and intrigued. Furaha continued to stare at Kaku, waiting for her to continue. "Africa was built upon the backbone of strong African women who unified their people. Haya is an example of a black woman who lost her crown, as some black women have. A lot of our women have lost their crowns." "Kaku, why did you say black women and not African women? Aren't we Africans?" Furaha asked in curiosity.

Her grandmother interjected, "Yes, we are African, but we are also black. We have brothers and sisters in Europe. Blackness is our imprint, and "African-ness" is our DNA. Black is what connects us all to the motherland. Our bond is stronger than we think, Furaha. We are black, black is us, and we are Africans and Africa is us. Queen Aminatu stood up for her people. She did not give in to pressure. You must know not to compromise your power and identity to brutality or pressure. Do not sell yourself due to fear. A queen and warrior are supposed to stand with strength and dignity. She is ready to stand for what she believes in. The question is, what are you willing to fight for and stand for? Black women in history, African women in history, are the most lethal weapon to defeat colonialism, separation and racism." She paused then continued, "Sadly, we've collectively forgotten our history, so the black woman sees herself as if she is nothing. However, she is the past, present, and future of power and a danger to destruction. Some black queens like Haya have taken off their crowns because of lack of knowledge and stomped on it." Furaha began to understand why elders were called living libraries in her village. As she sat down next to Kaku's feet, she reflected upon her words, *"The mouth of an old person stinks but speaks ancient truth."*

In a lecture-like manner, Kaku's voice rose like a church pastor motivating a congregation, "Furaha, you must see the queen in yourself. If you don't, the world won't, as well. Know who Furaha is and define yourself. If you don't, others will tell you who you are. The loss of identity is the highest form of oppression." All the knowledge thrown at her filled every cell in her body.

Kaku smirked and asked, "Do you know Queen Nzinga?" Furaha shook her head, then Kaka continued, "She was a Queen in Angola during the 1600s. She fought against European colonization. She was the queen of the Ndongo and Matamba Kingdoms of the Mbundu people in Angola. She fought against the Portuguese who were trying to colonize Angola and Congo. She allied with the Portuguese to free her people. She was a great military strategist and a skilled negotiator who negotiated with the Portuguese to free her people. She stood up for her people. One thing that's important in life is to stand up for your people, Furaha. Don't fight your people. As our people say, when a house is on fire, and if the people in it are quarreling and fighting each other, the house will surely burn, and they shall surely die." The skies turned darker, embellishing itself with stars of all sizes. The moon hovered over them, giving them the light they needed as their electricity went out. "The black woman, the African woman, has always fought for the liberation of their people. Imagine if we still supported each other and held each other to fight the real enemy. Look at the courage and fight of Pauline Lumumba. The wife of Patrice Lumumba. After the assassination of our Father of Independence in 1961 in Congo DRC, and after his body was destroyed, Pauline Lumumba, a humbled woman born in 1937 in Kasai, marched in Leopoldville, present-day Kinshasa to mourn and protest his death. People followed her and mourned and marched with her, which sparked many movements and protests. Some thought she was crazy, but the small thing she did by walking bare-chested sparked protest. The black woman has always fought for justice and her people, but we forgot who we are, Furaha. However, you cannot forget who you are. You must know your history to know who you are and where you are going, Furaha. You are a strong and courageous woman, just like these women.

Kaku dwelled in silence once more, then eventually changed the topic, "A race who doesn't respect their women, doesn't respect their future." Furaha pondered on that last statement. She wasn't sure why the phrase haunted her mind and turned her bones cold. Furaha's uncles, aunties, and cousins came into the compound, and an uncle expressed, "We did not find food," while other family members told jokes and stories. "Betu'abe Kaku," they all greeted Kaku. "Betu," Kaku responded. They also greeted Nkoko as he walked in.

76

They all circled the place, which normally had charcoal brazier. Maman Beya, Furaha's aunt and Kaku's daughter, went into the house and brought more charcoal for the fire. Mbiya, Maman Beya's older sister, grabbed the rocking chair for Nkoko as she was told and sat it next to Kaku. Nkoko's face filled with delight, but stomach growled with hunger. Uncle Fiston sluggishly walked into the veranda and greeted everyone and bowed his head as a way to show respect, "Jambo, Jambo. Give me a seat, please." Maman Beya grabbed a chair and placed it within the perimeter of the circle.

They all sat in hunger but enthusiastically told stories as if the passages filled them up. Penda sat next to Furaha, then placed a corn husk into the brazier until it became fiery. Once she started waving it from side to side, Eric furiously scowled , "Penda, stop that, don't you know that summons demons to come into the compound! Demons are not welcome here. So, Stop."

After Eric alluded to the myth, Uncle Fiston smirked while recalling a story he once heard before. It was as if stories were warm baked bread ready to be eaten. He cleared his throat then proudly began, "There was once a man who was in love with a beautiful young girl named Bibubwa, who lived in his village. Bibubwa was a beautiful young maiden seeking marriage. One day, a gentleman came to propose to her. He vowed to love her, and this was his vow speech, 'Bibubwa, I love you deeply. I adore you, and from the first time I saw you, my heart became imprinted. I may not be as rich as my neighbor, Dibwa, but I will love you.' Bibubwa's heart was happy. She cried, hugging the man. After some moments, she finally said, 'Please, if you deeply love me the way you say you do, introduce me to your neighbor Dibwa, so I can marry him." They all laughed hysterically as if they never heard a joke before. The story and laughter seemed to have filled them because their stomachs stopped growling. They told stories all night until each person was embraced by the winds of sleep. After each person fell asleep, Kaku took a container of water and poured it on the charcoal brazier to quench the fire, then headed to sleep.

The night flew like a jet leaving a trail of white smoke in the sky. As usual, Furaha stared blatantly into spaces, windows, and walls to pass through the night, which seemed like an eternal pillory. She could not move because six bodies were lying in the same bed as her, amicably sleeping. She mentally wandered through the night until morning came.

Kaku stayed true to her routine and rose from her slumber early in the morning before anyone else. Furaha listened to the distinct pouring of water in a bucket by Kaku and the footsteps of Kaku as she took the bucket into the shower latrine. Furaha paid attention to all the sound effects of Kaku's movement until she went back to her room, and a cockroach crawling on the wall caught her attention. Roaches were honorary residents of the compound.

The morning was in full swing once the rooster crowed, welcoming the morning and awakening souls. Furaha rose from the bed after rejection from sleep. Then she took her miswak toothbrush, poured water into a mug, and strolled to the back of the house to brush her teeth. While taking care of her gorgeous smile, she felt that this day might differ from her typical one.

Part 2

Around midday, Nkoko's childhood friend, Diba, and his son, Benga, came with a sack of tomatoes, matembele, spices and a bag of fufu. They all welcomed him with open arms, hopeful that he traveled from Mbuyi-mayi to Lubumbashi to deliver food for them. Nkoko thanked him, blessed him with ancestral blessings, which Nkoko proclaimed to follow Diba all the days of his life. Diba accepted the words of blessings, for when an elder or an ancestor speaks, the heavens listen. When an elder blesses, earth heeds. When an elder cries, divinity responds. Diba revealed that his arrival was to bring the food they grew in their farm. "We came to bring some food we have in our farm. I know how hard the economy is." Nkoko took the food into the veranda and summoned the household to come cook as Nkoko walked Diba to the avocado tree. "Mbiya," Nkoko summoned. "Please give us an extra chair for Diba."

"Baba, it is fine. I am not staying long. I will stand," Diba asserted. "My house is your house. It is your home. You came a long way. You must eat and rest. You can go back to Mbuji-Mayi tomorrow after the sun rises. I insist. Come and enjoy this with us. We slept with no food yesterday. Our people say, where the rain falls, there is no hunger. You have brought us rain. Last week we went three days without food but mangoes" Nkoko explained with such sorrow in his voice. "Nkoko, things are difficult, but it will be well," Diba interrupted. Mama Mbiya brought the chair, and Diba sat down under

the avocado tree next to Nkoko while Benga followed Maman Mbiya
to the veranda.

"Asante mama," Diba whispered. Maman Mbiya walked back to
the veranda where everyone gathered around the charcoal brazier,
some blowing into the charcoal to ignite all the charcoal, others
cutting the matembele, others washing the *enswa,* getting it ready for
cooking. Kaku sat in her rocking chair, directing people if she saw
that the seasonings were not enough or if the water was too much.
Timba placed a pot on the brazier, poured palm oil into the pan, and
waited for the oil to be hot. When it became hot, he added salt, which
he measured with his eyesight, and added the matembele. The palm
oil simmered, bubbling into the matembele. "Kaku, who was King
Leopold of Belgian?" Furaha asked, reminiscing of the former day's
lecture from Mr. Tshisengu.

Kaku looked at Furaha and back at the pot on the brazier, then
uttered "Leopold was not a king as some may call him, because a king
builds the strength of a people, not destroy people. Leopold was the
so-called King of Belgian who took Congo from 1885 to 1908, by the
permission of the Berlin Conference in 1884. This conference had all
the European powers choosing which African region they wanted to
dominate. They split Africa like a birthday cake, poked forks into it,
and shared it. Leopold chose Congo and convinced the conference
holders that he wanted to explore the Congo basin for charitable
reasons. This snake colonized our country, deprived us of our dignity,
stripped us of our honor. He killed our brothers and our sisters. More
than ten million people died under his colonial rule. A holocaust
unspoken of because the life of a black soul seems like a vapor in the
hands of time." Kaku sternly gazed at Jibu, Mama Mbiya's eight-

year-old son running in the compound, touching the rubber vines engulfing the compound. Jibu cut a piece of the rubber vine tree and the milky latex leaked over the rubber vine tree, and Jibu's hand touched it.

When he rubbed his eyes, the milky latex hurt his eyes, and he screamed in agony. Maman Mbiya ran to attend to him and asked, "Jibu, are you okay?" Diba interjected, "Wash his eyes with water." Kaku tapped her right foot for a few seconds then fretted, "Those tears are not foreign in this compound. Nor are they foreign with the same rubber vine." "Kaku, he's a little boy. Why are you making a big deal of this situation?" Maman Mbiya asked angrily. Furaha stared at Maman Mbiya then back at Kaku. Kaku shrugged off the question and exclaimed, "Furaha, during Leopold's rule, our people were enslaved in their own country. Leopold was not the father of civilization in our country. He destroyed Congo. Leopold used brutal systems of exploitation to take our wealth. He had a group that would beat, torture, and murder men, women, and children. The men were told to go find rubber trees and take latex for the Belgian. They took care of others but never had time to care of themselves. Congolese people were made to collect rubber for different Belgian companies. Each family was given a quota to meet. If they did not meet the rubber quota, they were sentenced to death, hands cut off, legs cut off, and held as a memorandum to instill fear in other Congolese. Leopold's soldier brought him baskets of chopped hands, and he would rejoice in the misery of our people. My grandmother's brother was a victim of this massacre. His son's hand was chopped off because he never met the quota. His wife was held hostage, raped, and tortured to death. That evil man killed more than ten million of our brothers and sisters. Among them were our family members. He burned the villages of my fathers. My father, whose name was Boyeka, was also a victim of this atrocity. They killed us for rubber and built their wealth upon our misery. Jibu's cry is only a mimic of the pain that our people endured, but we cannot allow that pain to be our barrier to move forward. For the pain and destruction they have caused us, they can never give us enough reparations, apologies, and sympathy that will fix our broken past."

The aura in the room waned, and calamity flew in when Maman Mbiya's sister, Nzita, was seen idly roaming outside the compound with a marred face. Maman Mbiya, along with others rushed to where she was to tend to her. Before they reached her, she dropped to the dry dirt hurting legs more. When her siblings Anto and Maman Mbiya reached out, Anto angrily asked, "Nzita, what happened? Did he do this to you again?" Nzita's husband was abusive, and they knew this. He would beat her, spill salt in the cracks of her wound, then laugh at her when she would scream.

"Did he do this?" Maman Mbiya emphasized, holding onto Nzita's arm to keep her from falling. Maman continued when she realized Nzita's lips swelled and she wrestled to keep her eyes open, "This must change. He can't continue to hit her like this. How could a man do this to the mother of his children? Nkoko, come and see this!" Maman Mbiya roared

One of Nzita's children that stays with Nkoko and Kaku came closer to mother and asked, "Mama, are you okay? He did this to you?" Nzita's children stayed with her parents because of how abusive Nzita's husband was. They were afraid to return to their father's house.

Nkoko began shouting, then grabbed a fufu stick and walked out of the compound to go beat the man who attacked his daughter. Kaku shouted, "Tatu, please stop! You can't solve this with violence. The elders must know of this."

"What will the elders do but send her back?" Maman Mbiya exclaimed. "The elders would rather see her miserable, but in her own husband's house."

Everyone in the compound tried to stop Nkoko from acting out of rage, but Nkoko kept shouting. "Tatu!" Kaku called out to Nkoko respectfully. Tatu was a word Kaku used to show her husband Nkoko respect as the man of the house. Nkoko calmed down and walked back to his seat under the avocado tree. "Mamu," Nkoko, respectfully called Nkaku . "Please, give me water." Mamu was the word Nkoko used to show respect to Kaku for being the mother of the house. This was the way of the elders in their tribe.

"Eyo papa," Kaku replied and fetched water for Nkoko. After Kaku walked back to her seat, close to the charcoal brazier with all her children and grandchildren, silence clung, and all one could hear was the coal in the charcoal brazier crackling in the fire. While treating Nzita's wounds, Anto would say, "It is sad that women are not respected anymore in our culture. Hitting the same woman that gave you children is self-hatred. He needs to be taught a lesson."

Mbiya nodded, then added, "Some men do not understand the damage they cause on a woman." Nzita continued to sob, revealing more wounds and bruises under her shirt and all over her legs. She cried in agony when Mbiya used hot water and a rag to massage her body.

Nzita began venting about her husband's constant abuse and how that led to her miscarriage. Her husband kept her locked in the bedroom for days without food, as he would go entertain other women. He threatened to kill her if she spoke of the situation to people or ran. Nonetheless, Nzita ran for her life after he threatened to take the remaining children to the village and marry a second wife.

Nzita caught her breath and with a low inaudible voice she lipped, "One day, he came home drunk while I was preparing food for him. He was accompanied by another woman, and he became angry that I was at home. This man had the nerve to ask me why I was home. I told him I lived there, and that I was cooking. He thought I was disrespecting him in front of the woman, so he walked towards me, threatening me. When I reacted, he picked the pot of food on the brazier, held my neck, and pushed me to the ground. He told her to go wait in the room while he beat me. I bled through my nose and my mouth. Plus, he kicked my stomach multiple times, and I almost died. While I was on the ground crying, I knew my tears were for my lost child. I did not want to run away because I cannot leave my marriage. Marriage is sacred."

Anto quickly responded, "Well, he isn't treating marriage like it's sacred. Nzita, you cannot go back there!" Anto defensively bawled, "No, I must go take care of my husband. I cannot leave him on his own. It is my duty as a wife to take care of my husband. I-" Anto cut her off and cried, "And it is his duty as a husband to take care of his wife, but he beats you. Your husband is not your baby to always take care of" Anto dropped her head in defeat, "I cannot leave my marital house. You know our culture. The elders will talk." Anto put her delicate hands over hers and compassionately implored, "Let them talk. You will rather come back in a coffin than alive. That guy will kill you. It's obvious he doesn't care about you. He impregnated you, destroyed your life, now wants other women. People will always talk. You can cut your head and present it in front of people, and they will still talk."

In a brainwashed manner, Nzita responded, "Anto, you don't understand. I vowed to serve him." Mbiya inquisitively asked, "So you would rather die serving him?" Without thinking, Nzita answered, "Yes. I was waiting to just die. That was my only escape. If I died, I would've died in my husband's house, which is better than running away. If I died, my story would have remained that I was still married until my death. I lost hope, but I continued to fight."

Everyone else looked at each other and knew they were fighting an uphill battle to convince Nzita to go against cultural values. Mbiya slurred, "You cannot continue to fight a battle you know you won't win. You have to leave. You've prayed, fasted, did everything to change him, but you can't change a man who sees nothing wrong with himself and how he is treating you. You have to look after yourself, Nzita.

Nzita didn't strengthen her case for staying when she brought to light her husband pouring boiling water on her leg, which bound her to a wheelchair for three weeks. In a confused manner, Anto asked, "Why did you not come here, Nzita eh?" She looked up for the first time during the conversation and whispered, "I did not want my marriage business to be heard on the street. You have to protect your marriage." "You protect what's good and expose what's spoiled," confessed Mbiya.

Uncle Fiston stood in front of the house door, listening to his sister Nzita. He barged into the room and snarled, "We can blame that man all we want, but Nzita is also to blame! Why would you go to the house of a man who beats you? And you still return –eh. It's her fault that she is beaten." "Fiston!" his sister Maman Beya asserted. "How is it her fault for caring for a man she vowed to serve? She is married to the man and being a wife to him." He raised his voice and stuttered, "Why be a wife to a man who has shown you that he does not want to wife you? Nzita, this better be the last time you go over there! I don't understand some of you women. You put yourself in these situations and blame the guy. Nzita, blame yourself. This is nonsense. You knew how he was, but you still went back. You are very stupid, very stupid."

Kaku remained in her chair while she stirred the pot of food and listened attentively to her children. "No, no, Nzita was beaten for her stubborn head," exclaimed Ngondu. "You know how Nzita is. She was probably disrespecting Biselele, disobeying him, and not performing her duty as a woman. See, if you cook for a man, clean his clothes, obey him, submit to him, serve him, he will not treat you like this. You were probably acting like a man to him. Men don't like that. Men like control." Uncle Fiston nodded proudly and co-signed that message.

"You see, my husband. I treat him well. Before he comes home, his food is ready. When he is taking a shower, I prepare his clothes. I serve him. If he says something, I say yes. I don't argue with him. If he says I am wrong, even if I am right, I keep my mouth shut. That's what you must do to keep your marriage. Don't let these people fool you," Ngondu continued to assert her point.

"Please tell your sister, Ngondu," Uncle Fiston interceded. "If she wants to keep her marriage, she must follow these principles. They have worked for ancient marriages. She cannot break the rules of marriage and expect to make a happy home." Nzita sat quietly, and Furaha gazed at the whole scene unfolding. Normally when situations such as this come up, the kids are told to go elsewhere. However, the young ones stayed on the scene for this.

Why do some men feel the need to assert dominance and superiority in such a way? Furaha thought. She vowed never to marry and lock her heart with resentment and anger. What happened to Aunt Nzita will never happen to me because I will never marry, she vowed.

"Ngondu, shut up. You are a puppet to your husband. You are a mother to a boy you never gave birth to. You can do all those things and still get beaten. It's not about how well you treat him. Some men will still treat you like nothing," Mbeya exclaimed. Ngondu rolled her eyes and smacked her mouth.

The tantrum continued to burn the spirit of joy before Nzita came with the news. The night turned colder. An abnormal silence befell the family as they all ate their meal. After their meal, they all went to sleep, but Furaha tried sleeping but couldn't. Nzita woke up in the middle of the night and sobbed. Her stomach and spirit ached.

She thought a breath of fresh air would help but was sadly mistaken and continued crying. Furaha's energy woke Kaku up. After she was awakened, Kaku woke up, took the bamboo mortar and crushed herbs, made a drink, and then gave it to Nzita. It was bitter, and Nzita wrestled with swallowing the substance. After a while, her stomach pain ceased. Mbiya took her back into the room, and she slept for the rest of the night.

The night turned into sunrise, and the day proceeded. Hunger befell the household. Nkoko went out to fetch food and seek a job. He knew that Congo's economy plunged into a decline, causing many people to lose their jobs. He was one of the victims that lost his factory job due to the decline. He knew that there was no hope for him to receive a job, but he went to seek it anyway. It was hard for people to find employment or any source of income. Even with his hair grayed, and a slight slouch from age, he still took the responsibility to seek a job to take care of his family.

Kaku woke everyone early in the morning after Nkoko left before sunrise. She urged everyone to grab tools to go by the river in Bukama for fish and mineral stones. "Kaku, it is too early, and that is a long journey. Why are we going there?" Penda pleaded, rubbing her eyes. "Just grab the tools and prepare yourself to go there to dig and fish. You will find food in Bukama," Kaku muttered. They all grabbed knives, placed them in their bags, slipped on their torn shoes, took the change that Kaku managed to get from Diba, and ran to the marketplace to catch the vans for Bukama.

The market was noisy and filled with enthusiastic vendors luring people to buy their merchandise. "Kababale for 8390 Franc," a woman repeated these words while chasing away flies with her hand fan. Uncle Fiston gazed at the dried catfish, wishing he had enough money to buy one for home. They waited at the bus stop, which was hawked by taxis and chauffeurs yelling, "We will give you the best service!"

Uncle Fiston spoke for the group and said, "Hello, we are looking for a chauffeur from here to Bukama," "Ah Ndio, watu wangapi?" the chauffeur inquired. "It's six of us," Uncle Fiston responded, then pointed at Penda, Furaha, Benga, Ngondu, and Nzita's two children. The cab driver compassionately nodded his head then they squeezed into the muggy and overcrowded van alongside other passengers.

The chauffeur yelled, "Okay, Twende, Twende!" Then banged on the side of the van, honked, and drove off as the van emitted smoke. The chauffeur dropped off everyone and continued to Bukama. When they arrived, the chauffeur let them off and asked for an extra tip due to the long journey and bumpy road. Uncle Fiston pleaded with him because they only had enough for *aller-retour*. The chauffeur agreed and pulled off. Then the family journeyed by foot to the village of Bukama.

They saw how desolate Bukama was compared to Lubumbashi. It seemed like Bukama still held onto the effect of Belgian Colonization. The children ran freely in the sand, and mothers hovered in front of their homes, grinding grains in their bamboo mortars and carrying their children on their backs. "May God help Congo," Uncle Fiston commented. They all continued to gaze at the joy on the children's faces as they played with a piece of metal and stick and pretended it was a car. "This area in Bukama used to be a camp ran by Belgian soldiers. This is where some Belgian soldiers would cut the women's breasts and leave them to die on the streets. Shoot the kids, snatch them from their parents, and cut off their right hands. This is where some of their camps held Congolese people hostage. Their leader would make people carry him as if he was a divine king."

Uncle Fiston gazed at the river and summoned them to walk towards it. When they arrived at the river, Uncle Fiston tried bargaining with a man that worked on a dugout canoe to ride for half the price. They finally allowed him to board, handed him a paddle, and he began rowing. Most picked a place along the outskirts of the river and started digging. Some began walking into the nearby forest for vegetables, and others waited by where some canoes were parked. Furaha searched for dark stones because she remembered Kaku saying, *"These stones grow underneath the ground, mostly by rivers."*

She also remembered Kaku saying, *"Congo is blessed and cursed with them. They grew in the ground like sand on a vast sea."* She was puzzled *how something can be a blessing and a curse at the same time?* She continued digging with her grandfather's ancient Congo scabbard knife. "Furaha!" Benga called out, returning from the nearby forest. Furaha looked at him silently, waiting for him to continue with his thought. "Can you come with the basket? I found some lenga lenga." Furaha got up with the basket and followed Benga into the forest to pick up the vegetables. Furaha picked as much as she could and filled her basket. Benga smiled as she hustled, then led her to another site that had mushrooms.

Furaha gazed at the mushrooms and knew they were Kaku's favorite. She picked until she couldn't anymore. Once they were finished, Benga suggested that they sit by a log. Furaha conceded, then he giggled, "Come, sit down and rest. We will go in a couple of minutes once everyone is done, okay?" Furaha reluctantly sat next to him and gave Furaha some palm fruit. They sat in silence, chewing on the palm fruit. "So, how is your school?" Benga asked. She answered, "My school is great, but I can't go back because I can't pay my school fees," "What about your papa? Does he not send you money?" Benga questioned.

Furaha unconsciously grew emotional and responded, "He does sometimes. I know he will send it if he has it. I just hope it's soon. Kaku begged my Professor to allow me to stay in the class, but I don't even have a book to take notes in." "So, how do you take notes?" Benga interjected. She shamefully lowered her head, "I stole Penda's drawing book, but Kaku saw it and yelled at me. Now I can't use it anymore."

Benga looked at Furaha with a tin of passion in his eyes and tittered, "I can help you pay your school fees. You know me and Papa Diba have a farm in the village that we use to sell things and make money. I'd love to help." Furaha tearfully accepted it. While she imagined herself finishing her education, Benga slid his hands across her undeveloped breasts. Then his hand traveled down her thighs, tracing invisible lines.

"Uncle Benga!" Furaha squealed. Benga silenced her and continued, "I can help you pay your school fees. Just don't tell anybody about this, sawa. If you do, then I won't pay for your school fees." He continued caressing her, speaking to her in a profane language that perpetrated her innocence and childhood. Benga proceeded to kiss her neck as Furaha cowered in disgust. He claimed this was a way for her to say Asanti to him. When Benga's hand caressed her, he summoned her to get up, as it was getting late, and he wanted to avoid suspicion of his perverted acts. Furaha straightened herself and walked out of the forest with Benga. Her body felt as though someone pierced her with nails. She felt like vomiting but kept reminding herself of her overdue school fees.

Uncle Fiston emerged from fishing, holding onto a basket of tilapia. The rest of the family came in with what they found. Some extracted dull metallic stones, which Uncle Fiston claimed were coltan. Furaha was unsure of why these stones were so precious. Ngondu filled her plastic bag with the stones, and they all walked a mile to wait for the bus alongside the main road. A yellow van passed by, and Uncle Fiston spoke to the chauffeur, bargaining for a reasonable price. He covered the tilapia with the plastic bags they brought to conceal the scent from permeating the van. The van was lively, with stories and priceless laughter, but Furaha remained buried in thought.

They arrived home, and Kaku welcomed them with chants in her native tongue. Kaku glanced at the bag of stones and summoned Fiston to go to a mining site with the others the following day. "Ngondu, Mbiya, please prepare the mbisi for cooking. Anto, please grind the pondu in the bamboo mortar." Anto did as she was told. They all gathered around the veranda to prepare supper. Nkoko returned, walked into the compound with a face filled with disappointment. Kaku took a rocking chair and placed it underneath the avocado tree in the compound. She sat by him on a mat and heeded his voice.

Ngondu started the fire, Mbiya seasoned the mbisi, and Anto finished crushing the pondu. Beya brought the pots for the food, and they began cooking. Diba walked into the compound and walked towards the avocado tree. A chair was brought to him, and he sat next to Nkoko. Nzita slept on a yellow plastic rug, next to Kaky, shivering under her blanket. It was not cold, but she shivered, at times, waking from her slumber screaming, "He's here, he's here! Please don't hurt me!"

Kaku hugged her while humming her favorite lullaby. Beya exclaimed, "The scar that man left on her is not going away anytime soon. Kaku, we have to take her to the hospital." "We will use the money we get from selling the mangoes and stones tomorrow to take her to the hospital," Uncle Fiston exclaimed. They all watched the startling sight of their sister trembling and screaming in and out of her sleep.

When the food was ready, they woke Nzita to eat. She was reluctant, but Kaku helped her finish the food. After supper, they all slept. The night terrorized Nzita. Each second of darkness triggered the horrific beatings and bleedings she experienced. She silently murmured, "mtoto wangu, mtoto wangu." Her voice rose as her hands began fighting the air. The house woke up, and Beya yelled, "Nzita! Nzita!"

Nzita awakened with a shirt drenched in sweat and a face filled with tears. Beya took her outside for fresh air, and Kaku crushed some herbs for her. She swallowed the herbs and cried crocodile tears for her lost baby. She desperately asked, "Where is my baby? Mtoto wangu, where is my baby?" Nzita's mind buried her in a nightmare she couldn't wake up from. She couldn't close her eyes without envisioning the kicks that killed her baby and the blood flowing from her body. The flashbacks seemed so surreal. Each thought haunted her. When she was taken outside, she checked around the compound for her husband. She felt a dark shadow hovering over her calling her worthless, nothing, disgusting, and spitting on her.

Sleep eloped from the house. Nkoko awakened, took his machete, and walked out of the compound late in the night to Nzita's husband's house. "Baba, where are you going?" Anto asked. He answered, "To show that stupid man a lesson. My daughter is suffering because of him. I will kill him." Uncle Fiston added. "He deserves to die, look at Nzita," while pointing at Nzita's demeanor, as she tightly gripped Kaku's arms.

Each breath became heavier and more strained than the next. Beya calmed Nkoko, took the machete, and walked him inside. The night passed with a bitter scent of burning flesh. The family tried sleeping but couldn't. The sun came out and welcomed the family, reducing the aura melancholy. They woke up early, and Nzita was given a mat to lay outside. While Fiston, Anto, and Beya prepared for their journey to the mining site in Kasai, Furaha and Penda stayed with Kaku, asking about the stones. "These stones are called coltan. We hold a vast amount of them underneath our ground. They make the phones you see plus cars and computers we hear about. They are vital," Kaku stated.

Diba rose from his slumber with a cup of water and a miswak brush for his teeth. He interrupted and stated, "You know these stones are not just stones. They make the world electronic as we know it. Congo is blessed and cursed with 80% of it. It should bless us, but it has caused numerous problems and solved none. It is a curse of paradise, plus a parasite that has infected our economy and our country with corruption. It's our death sentence from which I pray God delivers us from." Uncle Fiston walked out, and Anto and Beya prepared themselves to leave. They secured the coltan inside a backpack and went on their journey to the mining site in Kasai, by the Bushimaye River to sell the minerals.

On their way, they told stories, folklore and sang songs in Tshiluba and Lingala to entertain themselves. They laughed at jokes, roasted each other, and retold Kaku's stories. When they arrived at the mining site, they were taken into a little room where they displayed the coltan for inspection and pricing.

One of the workers claimed it was real and weighed five kilograms. Fiston looked at his siblings, Beya and Anto, to determine what price they would charge the worker. "Four hundred dollars," Anto murmured to Fiston. Fiston looked at Anto undoubtedly but agreed. They voiced their price, then were bargained to $350. The chief of the workers sent one of the workers to give Anto and Fiston the money, and the exchange happened smoothly.

They took another hour and a half to arrive home, this time using transportation. Their joy from the profit lit a spark of excitement once they returned to the compound. They peeked at the avocado tree, glancing at Nkoko distraught while resting his head against the back of the chair, staring into the dull avocado leaves. "What happened to Baba?" Fiston asked Kaku. "Nzita was taken to the hospital by Diba. She was taking a shower, and we heard her collapse. Baba has been sad since she left." Uncle Fiston placed the bag on the floor and rushed to the hospital. Kaku summoned Anto and Beya to take Furaha and Penda to the marketplace to buy some Ntaba and biteku-teku. Furaha and Penda rearranged themselves and strolled out the house with Beya and Anto.

They walked to the market and spotted an array of vendors selling clothes, peppers, mangoes, vegetables, meat, and fresh fish. One of the street entrepreneurs yelled, "Maman Beya, come see these peppers. They are fresh and were picked yesterday. You will love them. They will make your soup and food taste good." Beya and Anto kept strolling through the streets of the market until they found what they were looking for. They purchased the biteku-teku and the ntaba along with ingredients needed to make the dishes.

On the way back home, Penda and Furaha met their friends three blocks from the compound and decided to join a double dutch session. "Furaha, get in," one of Furaha's friends asserted. While jumping, they sang a song in their mother tongue as she jumped up to the rhythm. The evening turned dark as Furaha and Penda continued to play with their friends.

When the dull streetlights cut on, Furaha and Penda ran back to the compound. Everyone back home was in the veranda cooking and listening to stories. Beya and Ngondu were still at the hospital with Nzita. The uncles and aunties stayed telling stories. Diba cleared his throat,"The oldest civilization is Egypt. Egypt birthed Africa's civilization, dating back to 3100 BC. They introduced science and math. The first humans were there." Fiston interjected Diba before he continued with his thoughts, "Well, it is true that Egypt holds one of the oldest civilizations in Africa, but there are civilizations that precede Egypt that people do not talk about much. You see, in 1960, there was a Belgian archeologist whose name was Jean De Heinzelin. He found a mathematical artifact called the Ishango Bone here in Congo. Archeologists believe this bone dates back to 20,000 BC. This means it existed way before the Egyptian empires and a part of African civilization began in Central Africa. It was found in a small community near the Semliki river among the remains of a settlement buried by a volcanic eruption. The Ishango Bone was part of the Upper Paleolithic era and the second oldest mathematical tool containing the number system. They believed that the notches on it were to count the menstrual cycle of women, but some say it was a lunar calendar. Nonetheless, it was among the first tools used to prove the existence of civilized people in Africa and Central Africa." "What was the first oldest mathematical tool, Uncle Fiston?" Jibu asked. He answered, "It is the Lebombo bone which dates back to 35,000 BC in Swaziland." "So civilization began in Africa?" Benga asked. Uncle Fiston's eyes widened, then he responded, "Yes, you know people found the Omo human remains in Ethiopia. Initially, the scientists thought they were 130,000 years old. However, after doing more research, they found that it was 195,000 years old. Africa is the cradle of civilization and humans. They also found a dagger that was used 90,000 years ago for fishing in our country. We created advancement, technology, architecture, and other systems before anyone else." "So what happened? Why is Africa so poor now?" Furaha asked. Silence overcame the room, then Kaku leaned toward her and whispered, "Africa forgot her identity. We forgot who we are, where we came from, and where we stand. Greed became our friend, jealousy became our brother. We let the world tell us who we are while forgetting ourselves. That is the worst thing a person or a country can do because if you don't know who you are, someone else will tell you who. When the Europeans came to take what is ours, they knew our history, but they manipulated us to forget and disown it so that they could control us. We started to hate one another. We destroyed our empires. The Europeans found systems that were weak, and it was easy for them to control us." When the stories ended, they all grabbed plates and began to eat the cooked food while the conversation and jokes continued.

After the meal, they all washed their plates and cleaned the veranda. Uncle Fiston went to stand outside the compound with Diba in the foggy night to smoke a cigarette. The little boys stayed in the veranda playing the mancala game board. The women started to cornrow each other's hair. Penda sneaked out to go with her friends. Furaha stayed in the veranda, gazing at the mancala board game. She laughed at the guy's quarreling over the game. Benga continued to stare at Furaha.

The stares turned into uncomfortable smiles, and Benga rushed to where Furaha was sitting, "Do you like living with Kaku?" While holding back tears, she answered, "Yeah, I like living with her. I care about her a lot, but she is very sick, and no one knows because she doesn't want us to worry about her." Benga noticed her tears and wiped them away warily. He scuttled to Furaha closer and prattled, "I'm sorry for that. She's my Kaku too. Nothing will happen to her. I know I am just a family friend, but my father and Nkoko have been friends since childhood." Furaha knew Benga's words lacked something, but she couldn't put a finger on what it was.

Benga gestured for her to follow him, "I want to show you something. You seem very intelligent." Furaha hesitated but couldn't say no to an uncle because that was considered disrespectful. They walked, and Furaha came across a cockatoo flower she picked, but remembered Kaku's words. *"If you love a flower, you must water it, not pluck it. No flower should be plucked before its time."* She felt that she betrayed Kaku but plucked it anyway due to its beauty. Furaha loved flowers, especially cockatoos.

Furaha and Benga walked for a mile before returning home. Benga saw a mango tree filled with plumped mangoes and pulled Furaha underneath it. Benga forcefully yanked her under the fruitful tree and whispered, "Furaha, come here! You are so beautiful! Come closer." The dusky night concealed them, but the road light in the distance vaguely revealed the act. Furaha resisted, but Benga covered her with his overbearing power, and she felt her heart racing, but did not know why. He slapped the cockatoo flower to the ground, stepped on it, then unbuttoned his pants and pulled her dress. Benga's sweaty hand palmed her mouth and veiled her yells for help. "Shhhhhh, it'll be fine. You can't cry. I am your uncle. You can't tell anyone, especially Kaku. This will cause her to become sicker and die. You don't want that, okay?" Furaha grunted and tussled under the weight of Benga but couldn't move.

Penda's friend Imani was parading through the neighborhood and then she heard grunts, and saw figures under the mango tree. She paused and stared. Benga yanked his pants back to his waist, then took off running once he noticed a witness. Furaha squirmed, and limped away in the other direction while blood dripped from in between her legs. Imani gasped for air, her skin turned cold and she raced to deliver the news. When she met Penda, she fell into her warm arms gasping for air. When she finally became calm, she spoke, "I just saw Furaha with this guy in the back of your compound and her clothes were off, even the guy." Imani was known to be a gossiper, always twisting the truth, but she was very informed about things happening in the town.

"Doing what?. Your joking is becoming too much," Penda asserted.

"No, it's true, I swear to God. They were under the mango tree behind your house. They both ran when I spotted them. See," Imani muttered.

"I can't believe she would do that. I always knew she was not as innocent as she seems," Penda whispered.

"So what are you going to do now?" Imani asked.

"I won't tell anyone yet. I will ask her, Imani. If she lies, then I will tell Kaku," Penda uttered. "Okay, I have to go home. I will talk to you later. It is getting really late." Imani and Penda exchanged their goodbyes, then Imani skipped home.

Penda walked into the compound and found Furaha in the back of the house with water, cleaning herself. Penda glanced over at Furaha's dress and spotted patches of blood. Then saw blood dripping from between her legs. "Furaha, I know what you did. You were with a guy Furaha. You want to be with men, Furaha." Furaha turned away from Penda quickly, rattled by her reprisals.

"Who was the guy you did this with? Now look at you, bleeding on your clothes. Who was the guy you did it with?" Penda continued to press at Furaha, but it seemed like Furaha's vocal cords failed to explain the pain her body felt, and the disgust she felt. She sat on a brick while washing her feet. Silence fell amidst the two and Penda scrutinized her. "I will tell Kaku," Penda concluded. Furaha shook her head in disagreement. She managed to utter no, reminiscing of Benga's words. "If you tell Kaku, she might become sicker and even die." Penda continued threatening to tell Kaku, while Furaha continued to shake her head no. "If she dies, it will be your fault. You're having sex with a close family friend." Furaha's tears rolled down at a faster rate than earlier. She couldn't believe that her own blood turned her back on her.

Penda smacked her mouth then asked, "You know what? I won't tell anyone, but you have to continue doing my chores, or anything I say. If not, I will tell Kaku and the rest of the family. You know how shameful this will be. The perfect little angel Kaku loves is really a little monster." Furaha nodded helplessly, still holding on to the crushed cockatoo flower. Penda left to meet the others in the veranda. Furaha continued bathing herself while tears streamed down her eyes. She dug a hole and hid the flower underneath the ground. After bathing herself, she went through the back window into the bedroom and picked a white dress embellished with flowers. She threw the bloody dress into the trash bin behind the house and shamelessly walked to the veranda.

The blood flowed like a river, and she tried stopping it with paper towels. While grimacing through the night, she let out a silent, bitter sob that no one but God understood. The night haunted her. She felt hopeless and powerless. She tried to gain power from all the heroic stories of women Kaku told her but failed. Sometimes hopelessness is the only state that accepts you. Flashback of Benga's face nailed her soul and caused an eternal wound. Her life was now changed forever. She uttered a cursed prayer to God, but knew God doesn't answer to curses. But it became her life's mantra, "Dear God, please don't let her tell Kaku."

Please God don't let her tell kaku

Dear God, My eyes wandered as the night fell

Counting the roof tiles in my distraught and pain of yesterday's rile

Defeat fed to me in a violet pot

I've tasted the bitter tears rolling from my eyes

Tell me, what crime I committed,

Why guilt has come at my door.

What sin has my body committed that I live by the ropes of guilt tied around my neck.

Please God don't let her tell grandmother. Shut her mouth as you've shut raging waters. Is her death the answer to my prayers, is her crucifixion my liberation. God, Please don't let her tell kaku.

During the early hours of the morning, Diba and Benga left the house on their journey back to Mbuji-mayi. The whole family awakened to greet them and bless their journey. Furaha woke up and strolled outside with pain. She frowned at Benga, who seemed unbothered by his evil acts. He slickly smirked at Furaha then smiled at the family as he and Diba exchanged their goodbyes.

After a while, Beya rushed into the compound screaming in agony, with her hands on top of her head. When she arrived at the compound, she collapsed on the dusty ground, crying, while beating the ground. The family bombarded her with concern and questions. "Beya, what's going on?" Anto asked. She kept crying, screaming Nzita's name repeatedly. "What happened to Nzita?" Anto asked, helping her up. Beya refused to get up. After several drawn-out minutes of rolling on the ground like a fish with no water, she yelled, "Nzita died! The doctor told us this morning that Nzita died last night from internal bleeding." Tears were heard from Heaven's gates while they mourned Nzita's death.

Nkoko kept uttering her name in disbelief then left for the hospital, and Uncle Fiston. Kaku sat in the veranda crying for her daughter. She yelled out, "Why should my daughter die before me? I cannot bury my child! My child must be the one to bury me. No parent should bury their child." She cried until she got dehydrated, then took off her headwrap and revealed her gray hair. "When her husband beat, kicked, stomped, and punched her during her pregnancy it caused internal wounds and led to the miscarriage. She kept crying *mtoto wangu* last night, saying she wanted to go meet her baby," Beya exclaimed.

Nzita is now history. A closed story. Furaha sat shivering with fear, anger, and a concoction of emotions she did not understand. Nzita is penned in the history of those who lost their lives due to a culture that silenced them. Furaha feared that she would be next as blood trickled from a rape that others deemed justifiable.

The following days became dark and mourning-filled. Nzita's body was kept in the morgue as the whole town rampaged. Some blamed the late husband for being the cause of Nzita's death. Some blamed Nzita for causing her husband's rage. At a gathering to commemorate Nzita, one elder spoke up and bawled, "You see, I told you! Nzita was disobeying her husband. Why would a husband beat you if you don't disobey? Our elders say a woman is a baboon and her hands are eaten, and a man is like a baboon, and he eats with two hands. Young girls are not following traditions, and you see the result."

Many came to the compound to mourn the death of Nzita. Elders in the community sat in a circle discussing the wrongdoings and life experiences of Nzita. The women sat near the veranda on yellow rugs, legs crossed, and sobbed. Most of the women shivered. The elders discussed Nzita's death while Nzita's husband knelt before the elders.

Furaha sat by Kaku with a black headwrap on her head, still feeling pain between her legs. Furaha was unable to control her bladder. She gazed at Benga sitting among the elders speaking of the death. Agonizing pain boiled over while tears rolled down her cheeks, and she blamed herself for the ordeal. She silently prayed, "Please God, don't let them tell Kaku."

Nzita's husband knelt, and the elders' voices roared. The oldest of the group barked, "It is a shame that we let a man kneel down. He is a man. It is not our custom to belittle a man. My son standup!" He humbly stood up, fixed himself, and faced down. "The death of Nzita is not the fault of Biselele. A woman must heed to her husband's words. If the husband wants another wife, how does that concern the woman? Nzita killed herself. This boy does not have anything to do with this death," Nkolo's brother stated repulsively while chewing on his palm fruit.

The youngest of the group watched and exclaimed, "Elder Kisa, this boy deserves punishment. Biselele took Nzita alive from her parents' home. He must return her the way he took her, alive. Biselele, since you want to marry another woman, since you've abused her, bring her back to her parents' home alive, and we will give you your dowry, and you will be free to marry another woman." Nkolo's brother snapped back, "My friend, will you shut up! Nzita had health issues she inherited from her family. She killed herself. That is an abomination before our ancestors. It is an abomination before man. Do you even think the gates of death will accept her soul? She is aimlessly wandering in the spirit. Nzita killed herself. There is no blood on this man's head." The discourse intensified among the elders as the women watched in the distance, only muttering to themselves when certain elders spoke. Nkoko sat next to his brother, trembling with anger. He remained silent, allowing his brother to speak on his behalf.

One of the elders summoned a bucket of water for Biselele to wash his hands, to symbolize his innocence from the accusations. When the bucket of water was brought to the elder, he began enchanting in kikongo, swinging the bucket of water from side to side, walking among the elders. "My son, if you wash your hands in this water, you have agreed to plead your innocence. The blood of Nzita will not be on your hand, but if you kill her and you wash your hands in this water, the ancestors will punish you."

Uncle Fiston leaned against the pile of stacked red bricks near the veranda. He was tempted to pitch one directly at Biselele's temple, while his eyes twitched in disgust. Kaku was being held by two women who wept alongside her. Nzita's husband paused and gazed at each elder before dipping his hands in the bucket of water and washing them. After Biselele washed his hands, the elder took the bucket of water and spilled it in front of the elders. The elder bent down, picked up sand, and sprinkled it on the water he spilled. "You have declared yourself free. May the ancestors accept your oath and approve of your innocence."

There was an agonizing silence when Biselele walked away from the compound with his parents. The drummer's drumbeat, the ayele rang, and the ikembe sang, a powerful sound rose among the mourning people and sang in his native tongue,

"Sorrow befell me, my blood bleeds. My soul now wanders in the realms not known to me before Mama. I'm gone to see the dirt, as my body turns into ash, Papa. I've failed you, and my weight of sorrow befalls you. Ushale Bimpe, my family, no more will I see you. Eyowa, I'm gone. Mama, I'm sorry. Sorrow befell me, now my blood bleeds."

The man continued repeating the words, each time with piercing sorrow. Darkness fell, and the elders left the house, shaking their heads and spitting on the ground. Uncle Fiston started whistling in the corner. It is said that whistling will draw evil spirits closer, so the women gazed at him to stop. Some thought Uncle Fiston was summoning the evil spirit to avenge his sister's death. Kaku still sat on the yellow rug on the veranda floor, crying. Furaha sat next to Kaku, as she felt blood dripping between her legs. She couldn't walk or speak and kept praying that Kaku wouldn't find out. Furaha remembered her grandmother's stories about women who were courageous warriors. She thought about her favorite tale, which was about Kimpa Vita, the prophetess.

Kimpa Vita changed the course of history in the Kingdom of Congo. She led her own movement in a time period when the most powerful and wealthiest state in central Africa began losing its power. She was trained as a nganga, consulting the supernatural spirits, but received God and began changing the face of Catholicism. Kimpa Vita was a courageous woman who was not easily broken by the deeds of men.

Furaha conceptualized that you cannot control what the world does, but you can fight for what you believe and control what you do. Your power is yours. No one can take it if you don't let them. Not having anyone to turn to intensifies the trauma. While Furaha tossed and turned, she saw everyone sleeping but her. She started to fear sleep. What if he came again? What if he did it again?

Nzita stayed in the morgue for two weeks as the families argued about the burial and funding. Kaku's family caused havoc over Nzita's body. Nkoko's oldest brother requested the body for rituals.

106

"Since she is our blood, it will be the perfect sacrifice to the gods," Nkoko's oldest brother summoned. "Nzita will not be a wandering soul. She will have her resting home. We will not let you take our child," Kaku's words rang before both families. "Ipolo, haven't you taught your wife not to speak when the men in the family are speaking? This matter is not for a woman's voice. She disrespects our customs and traditions." Nkoko gazed at his elder brother speaking, attempting to silence his wife. "This is why we told you to marry in our tribe, but you went to marry outside. Now, look! Nzita's body will come with us to the village for rituals." "You will not take my daughter. My Nzita will not be your slave! She will rest in her burial home," Kaku chortled. "Ipolo, tell your wife. I am warning her. A woman should not have an opinion or voice in this matter. Dunia, obey our traditions before you bring a curse on you."

Furaha sat in the distance glancing at Kaku. Kaku seemed to display courage that empowered her. After the meeting, Nkoko's eldest brother summoned Furaha to grab the plate of palm fruits. Furaha ignored his request. He exclaimed, "Dunia, you see how you have spoiled these young girls in this family! Ipolo, warn your wife before she disgraces this family." Nkoko sat absently. He was torn between traditions and his wife's judgment. He remained silent for the following days. The death and burial of Nzita challenged customs and divided the family when Kaku decided to bury her child and sacrifice her soul's peace.

Months passed, and the mourning continued. Nzita's death left a wound that time couldn't heal. Nzita became a flower plucked prematurely. One cold morning, Benga brought a bucket of palm fruits, palm oil, cassava leaves, dry fish, and yams to comfort the family. The family welcomed him, but Furaha could not approach him. Her mind vividly relived the memories of that day. "Oh, thank you. May the ancestors bless you," Kaku blessed Benga in her native tongue. Watching oppressors receive praise is soul damaging.

The women took the food to the kitchen and began cooking. Uncle Fiston sat with Nkoko and Benga under the avocado tree watching people pass their house. It was a peaceful day, except for Benga's presence. The sun shined, leaves on the mango tree danced, and the sound of young girls playing the clapping game interrupted the stillness. Everything was tranquil until a young man came rushing into the compound.

Uncle Fiston inquisitively asked, "Masilika, what's going on?" He unsuccessfully tried catching his breath and pointed towards the compound entrance as if he was running away from someone. When he regained his wind, he shouted, "It's Biselele!"

Nkoko returned to his seat. Uncle Fiston looked at Nkoko and then back at Masilika and asked, "Ueh, what about him?" He checked his peripherals, "Blood, blood everywhere."

When the gasps halted and clouds thickened, a shout rose, "Biselele is dead. He was shot this morning, and his blood is everywhere. He was opening the door in the morning for one of the guys he worked with, and they shot him in the face."

The women were startled. Uncle Fiston asked Masilika to lead the way to Biselele's house. They ran to Biselele's home along with Benga. Some of the ladies ran behind Uncle Fiston to witness the scene. Furaha also ran, but she took a different path. She remembered visiting Biselele's house when her aunt Nzita lived there.

Uncle Fiston and Benga arrived at the scene, and they saw blood flowing from the threshold of the front door. The door was cracked, and the smell of death seeped out. Uncle Fiston and Masilika walked inside and unknowingly stepped into a puddle of blood. Once a crowd formed around the house, an elder shouted, "The ancestors have spoken!"

Furaha squeezed herself through the crowd and peaked at the cracked door. She saw Biselele lying down with his chest facing the white tile floor and eyes open. Blood spread all around his chest, and his head laid in a pool of blood. The blood trickled to the doorstep, and Furaha's right foot stepped in the blood. The blood felt warm yet cold. She stepped away from the door with blood dripping from the sole of her feet.

When she stepped away from the door, her right foot left imprints of Biselele's blood. The crowd slowly dispersed. Many felt it was the ancestor's rage. Furaha felt sick to her stomach and walked away from the house. After a few steps, she spotted Benga preying on a young girl in the distance.

Furaha clenched her fists, nostril flared, as a boiling fury swelled inside her heart. Her blood turned hot, and she felt her knees trembling. *When* she passed by Uncle Benga, he gazed at her with anger. She tried opening her mouth to yell, but no sound came out. The misperceived consequences of speaking out made her feel powerless. She wanted to undo her wrongs, but how can you undo the wrongs you didn't know you committed?

She ran towards the compound crying then stopped by a mango tree when she couldn't carry on. While the town cried for Biselele and Nzita, she cried over something she did not understand. She was unsure whether what Benga did was good or bad. Him offering the pay for school fees fueled her internal conflict along with her cultural pressures. She remembered her Professor's advice, "You cannot solve what you don't understand." Her heart went out for the other young girl Uncle Benga preyed on.

While getting dressed for Biselele's funeral, Furaha still felt a wrenching pain in her gut, but she continued to put on a strong facade. Sympathetic mourns disturbed Furaha's soul. She wondered, *Why are people crying over a man that beat Aunt Nzita to death?* He pled innocent before the elders and ancestors. Now they avenged Aunt Nzita's death by killing Biselele.

Furaha gazed at the women crying in awe. Then spotted Penda sitting in the distance by a branch with another girl. As she approached them, Penda's energy negatively shifted. Furaha felt distant from a girl that was once her sanctuary. Furaha greeted them both, but only the other girl responded. She tried sitting next to Penda, and Penda flinched. The other girl noticed and confronted Penda. "Penda, why did you do that? I thought she is your cousin." Penda rolled her eyes and condescendingly asked, "Which one, this one? Please, from where?"

The disrespect silenced Furaha and made tears run down her face. When Penda's friend confronted her about her mean act, she disowned Furaha and called her a prostitute. Then Penda told her version of what she saw the night of the incident. Penda's perspective included embellishments of her imagination. Her friend wiped Furaha's tears then responded, "Penda, sometimes things aren't as they look. Do you really think that Furaha did that?" "Ndio, Ni

Kahaba! She knows what she did. I will not be near Kahaba! I am leaving. Come find me when you finish."

"Furaha, you know our people will not understand. I know you did not do anything she said you did. I know how it feels to be in your position. A few months ago, I walked home from school with my friends. Eventually, they all left me to go to their homes, so I ended up walking alone. After a few blocks, I passed by an unfinished home. Before I knew it, a guy pulled me into the house and forced himself on me. He palmed my face so my yells couldn't be heard, but I bit his hands. I thought I'd be able to escape once I did that, but he hit my head, and blood leaked from my forehead. After a while, he wound up taking me down and raped me. Ubakaji. Alinibaka. Alinibaka sana." Furaha gazed at her smooth dark skin, high cheekbones and pondered what that saying meant. She could tell Furaha was still in need of upliftment, so her voice roared with fondness, "Don't ever for a second think it's your fault. What happened to you is a result of abused power and authority. What you experienced is called Ubakaji, and it's a result of people trying to assert their power over you to make you feel less than a human. The elders and men in our society feel entitled to females' bodies. They feel superior. When that happened to me, I went home and lied that I had gotten into a fight. I remained silent because of fear. Fear of being victimized, fear of losing my dignity, fear of losing everything. My fear fueled his strength. He would do it again because I was afraid to speak up. I hope you don't allow fear to silence you. I know it hurts you. It still hurts me. I don't think this pain will ever go away." The cycle will repeat itself until young girls and women refuse kanga motema. It'll stop once young girls and women find the power to speak up." Furaha recalled the stories of powerful African women who changed history by showing courage, and it awakened something in her soul.

After the conversation, Furaha wiped her tears, and forced herself to stand up despite her pain, then walked home. She did not know where the strength came from, but she vowed to break the cycle of silencing women. She realized it was not her fault, and what Benga did was not a good thing. He took advantage of her body, her innocence. She realized that it wasn't okay for Uncle Benga to do what he did, and she refused to allow another girl to be a victim. When Kaku told her that she was powerful enough to change history, perhaps this was what she meant. She knew that her voice would break the tradition of silencing Congolese and African girls. She encouraged herself to speak. "Furaha Sema, Furaha Sema," she repeated to herself.

She ran home, determined to break the cycle. She did not know how, but she knew that what Uncle Benga did hurt her, and she was determined to stop it from happening again. Furaha vowed to never remain silent again. She vowed never to die in silence like Aunt Nzita. She ran home, seeking freedom and justice.

"I was too terrified to speak, so I gave him power, but my fear is gone, and my mouth wants to speak."

Made in the USA
Middletown, DE
30 October 2021

50812903R00066